The
Town of
Whispering
Dolls

The Town of Whispering Dolls

stories

Susan Neville

FC2

TUSCALOOSA

FC2 is an imprint of The University of Alabama Press

Inquiries about reproducing material from this work should be addressed
to the University of Alabama Press

Book Design: Publications Unit, Department of English, Illinois State
    University; Director: Steve Halle, Production Assistant: Phil
    Spotswood
Cover image: Photo by Tracy Jentzsch; courtesy of Unsplash
Cover design: Lou Robinson
Typeface: Goudy Old Style

Library of Congress Cataloging-in-Publication Data
Names: Neville, Susan, 1951– author.
Title: The town of whispering dolls : stories / Susan Neville.
Description: Tuscaloosa : FC2, 2020. | Summary: "In The Town of
    Whispering Dolls by Susan Neville, the author creates stories that
    inhabit the rust belt of the early twenty-first century United States,
    where residents dream of a fabled and illusory past even as new
    technologies reshape their world into something new and deeply
    strange"—Provided by publisher.
Identifiers: LCCN 2019039454 (print) | LCCN 2019039455 (ebook)
    | ISBN 9781573661850 (paperback) | ISBN 9781573668873
    (ebook)
Subjects: LCSH: Middle West—Fiction. | Twenty-first century—
    Fiction. | Technological innovations—Fiction. | Social change—
    Fiction. | Psychological fiction.
Classification: LCC PS3564.E8525 .A6 2020 (print) | LCC PS3564.
    E8525 (ebook) | DDC 813/.54—dc23
LC record available at https://lccn.loc.gov/2019039454
LC ebook record available at https://lccn.loc.gov/2019039455

For Alison, Barbara, and Candace, who helped midwife this book.

Contents

*"Now Raggedy can think quite clearly!" cried all the dolls.
"My thoughts must have leaked out the rip before!" said Raggedy
Ann.*

—Johnny Gruelle

Foreword

Shelley Jackson

Listen: The dolls are singing.

They've taken off their heads. They like to do this sometimes. To stroll "with the rounded neck stumps in the breeze."

"How lovely it must be," adds Susan Neville.

Note this, first of all, then: Even if we are not the type to take our heads off, we can totally sympathize with the impulse. How lovely, indeed, "to not catch sign of yourself in passing windows!" To rid yourself of the petty parochialism of the self. Feel a cool wind slake the stump.

Then pick up a different head at the convenience store, when we're ready to take up the pain of thought again.

(The store also sells headache remedies, conveniently.)

Or to make some music. It is the wind over the neck-holes that does this. Something foreign blowing over and around us.

Such are the compensations for being no longer entirely human. They are strange but real. So while this book might sound a little pissed off at times, it's not didactic.

It is mordant. Which is to say, biting. Since one thing is clear, here in America's breadbasket: We eat and we are eaten.

It is possible to feel that this is even what we are for.

Parents feed themselves to their children. (As when giving suck. Or, here, wrapping up their body parts, crippling themselves piecemeal for Xmas gifts the kids don't even want.)

And feed on them in turn, "bite into their soft sweet arms." With "real hunger." With the tranquil cruelty of Greek myth, transposed into a midwestern America out of a ravenous dream.

This book hungers. For babies, eviscerated animals, a wine "the odd amber of animal eyes" (stop for a minute to listen to the music of those words), for delectable steering wheels, for the needle, love, sex, self-annihilation, the blood of Christ: "eating will always be a sacrament."

If a god haunts this book, it's a god with an appetite. Jonesing for whatever we can and must give up. Which in the end, of course, is everything.

We can't keep our homes, requisitioned by the army, then blown to smithereens. Can't keep our jobs, taken by robots, our factories, gone bust, our deserted churches, our poisoned earth, can't keep our children, turning into something we

don't recognize, can't keep our bodies, can't keep our memories, can't keep ourselves.

The hardships of a twenty-first century midwestern town figure
here as local representatives of a universal law of loss. They are
the local color on the slippery slope that living is.

For Neville, though, devastation is never without its beauty,
its allure, its strain of reckless glee, and its link to the sacred:
"the mystery of one thing becoming another."

"The fruit, the scattering of seeds."

So there's that, too—the ravening is terrible but glorious, a
faim fatale.

And after all we sometimes do desire our own destruction.
(The plague of dolls is spread, it would appear, by voluntary
acts.)

It's sometimes easier, as we've seen, to take your own head off.
To take yourself for a material thing, and relish your own lack
of agency.

(There is an addiction metaphor in play here, but let's not be
reductive. Who's not an addict?)

It's sometimes easier, too, to take others for material things:
your child or your parent, your lover or your enemy. The soldiers invite the lady dolls out to the army base, where they
play war games in the ruins of real houses.

But when living beings start becoming things, things begin to phosphoresce with secret life. A luminous table, an egg baby, a plume of toxic waste and mortal guilt.

Or a sentence with limpid, sometimes wild, prose.

Because writing itself forces mind and matter together. We play doll games with words. Breathing life into the dead things. Blowing across the neck holes to make the most terrible, beautiful music.

The
Town of
Whispering
Dolls

Grotto

You ask what makes the dolls sing? I'm not sure of the why, but I understand the how. I've seen it, and it's beautiful, and it breaks my heart. It requires only that they remove their heads.

As you know, the heads are empty. And so the singing comes from the emptiness at the base of the head, like wind blowing over the neck of a bottle. I can't say where the breath comes from, but it always comes.

The heads rest in the girls' laps, the heads tilted, eyes curtained, hands across the lips and the two painted teeth to preserve the tilt. Girls learn the tilt of the neck and pelvis. *Like this.* Move your hips *like this.* As long as there is a critical mass, the singing continues. It rises, falls and twists in the air, peppery and sad.

It takes place, this singing, in the grotto of the church. They sit in a circle around what was once the baptismal pool.

We live in a place where water shapes the topography of the land from underneath the surface, on a limestone sponge where most of the drama goes on beneath the ground. Dangerous roaring rivers, unmapped pirated streams, caverns filled with water, endangered blind albino cave fish beneath our unsteady feet. The grotto reaches down deep into a lost river that some say starts as ooze in a meadow and ends up as a tributary of the Mississippi. The river begins as a trickle of acid rain in the low regions before eating its way into cracks in the limestone like a crack in the tooth. A cosmic ooze.

Outside of town there's a bit of river at the surface, amber and chartreuse. And beyond that a swallow hole where the thirsty limestone gulps in the river, the hole a swirling pit of mud and debris where the river loses itself, disappearing underground. Right before it goes under, there's this piece of ground that looks like a solid raft of logs and sticks that you could walk across but which in fact is an illusion. Step on a timber raft and you will disappear.

The river appears again in the form of a spring in the base of the grotto. The church was built around the grotto. Outside the church the river takes a breath then dives underneath the ground again. Children are told that if they aren't very very good that the grotto will swallow them on the day of their baptism.

It's shallow, the grotto. Imaginative children see their faces rise up out of the pool when they lean over it. It frightens them as the singing dolls now frighten them. The dolls' long hair like seaweed. Some of the dolls are mothers. Their singing sounds like whale song, the eerie trilling somewhere between human anguish and joy.

It's easy to remove the heads, harder to lift and reattach them when the singing's over. They all attempt to replace their own heads, with varying success, and so they help each other like bridesmaids help a bride, arranging the veils of hair over the knees before the singing begins and helping place the head carefully on the neck stem when it's done. Before they begin their walk back out to the street, the eyes look forward and the hair is pushed back once again from the face.

Their eyes say *Don't let anything slip out* as the head is replaced: a secret lover's name, a theft, the memory of a stillborn child, the rape you didn't know was rape until later, things you couldn't tell your mother when you were a girl, the justice that could have been yours had you spoken then, had someone listened.

I am the mother of a girl who is now a doll, and I too was once a girl. Oh please forgive me for not speaking or not listening, for not *intuiting*. I cannot join you. I cannot save you. Cover the mouth, remove the head, wait for the air itself to pull it out of you. I know that in addition to the emptiness, your head has contained razor wire and string, needles and cracked glass. It requires care when unattached. You would not want to put your hand inside and rummage for seeds like you would a pumpkin. And at the end you want the head to reattach so the eyes can show a bit of blue or green, the spinal cord double knotted to the brain stem, the legs can move with purpose. There are times, yes, when you want to carry the head or put it on a shelf and be done with it, but there are other times when you want to form a choir.

I know that it feels good when the head and body go their separate ways. And sometimes the sound is so surprising it knocks you out. You sound like an angel when the wind blows across your cut throat. You feel as though you could fly.

So that, I suppose, is the why.

Here

Once the veneer factory closed and the moisture and termites turned the last few logs left in the lumberyard to splintery mush, everything started to deteriorate.

At one time there were stacks of walnut, cherry, oak, and maple out in the yard. I still remember the stumps of burls at the perimeter, like enormous mushrooms. Cancerous growths, they made the most beautiful swirls of veneer when they were dried and polished. Almost all cancer cells are beautiful under a microscope.

My husband and I spent our adult lives working in the mill. When the bark-denuded logs came to him from their soaking in the warm vats, they smelled like vinegar and pitch; they had been softened like butter. For years he sliced logs into pliant sheets, then put them on a drying bed. We made a good living here. I worked in the office, filling orders. We lived in a simple house. We walked to our jobs. He was a good man. We had four children.

The factory itself covered a block and looked like a rectangular tin can. There were a few daylight windows with green glass. Always the whining sound of the saws. It was comforting to me. Small Midwestern town. When the kids came home from school (consolidated, middle of cornfields) either one of us was home or we were at work three blocks away.

We were born here and my husband died here. I still live here.

We're underneath the clouds you fly over. Sometimes I look up at the jet trails following you, something that looks like a tiny silver wishbone glinting. That's you, up high on your way to someplace that isn't here.

There is no sign to our town on the interstate.

We're hemmed in by corn and soybean fields. The farms themselves are factories really, though they employ very few people. The owners live someplace far away. A few farm-workers come through on the migrant river in the summer. There are some smaller farms still: flax, hemp, strawberries. Farmers used to live on the farms, but it's become too dangerous. They live in the city and commute to their barns. Some mornings they spend calculating the cost of the overnight thefts.

We used to have a bank. The houses were painted then. There used to be flowers in the yards in the summer. Some had plastic flowers throughout the seasons, like a cemetery. Now and then a photographer will wander through here, looking for decay.

Why are they so fond of decay, these men and women with their cameras? Boarded-over churches, abandoned houses with sloping porches and shutters ripped down by the wind; overgrown bushes covering peeling doors, the occasional rowboat in the middle of a yard, a mattress on a porch, a wheelchair left in the middle of the street, trash.

Trash.

There's an empty lot with rusted trucks on the edge of town. We have decay in spades! I can't tell you how often it's been photographed, the decay. They show their pictures of our churches, barns, and trucks at art fairs. There are never any people in the pictures.

The first thing to go, it seems, is the veneer.

Sometimes veneer is beautiful, like fine upholstery covering a well-made chair or some extraordinary wallpaper in a well-made house. Sometimes it was less fine and covered plywood, glued-together sawdust rot.

We had four children and raised them here.

Sometimes people drive through on their way to the lake in Nineveh, pulling fishing boats behind their cars. They never stop on the way. My guess is you haven't been to Nineveh. The lake is weedy. You wouldn't want to swim in it, and there are car parts now on the lake's floor. Sometimes a reddish swirl of rusted sludge will ooze up from the bottom. Old chemicals from the veneer plant, I suppose. But the lake in Nineveh is stocked with bass, and a few old fishermen return there year after year.

When I leave here to visit one of the children I notice the ugliness when I return, sometimes a bit of strangeness, but my bed still feels good to me, and by the next morning the place

I remember has aligned itself again with the place that's here and there's rarely a sense of weirdness to me about the weather or the sidewalks, which is to say that I am home here.

Other things? There's an army base next to Nineveh. Mile upon mile of unexploded ordnance and active firing ranges. The base is dotted with fake Middle Eastern villages and the soldiers practice attacking the villages, stiff-walking, gun-led through the villages like fighters in a video game. Sometimes the army will put out an ad for civilians to dress up in head scarves and choir robes and pretend they're people being captured. The pay is minimum, and it's seasonal work. Sometimes the big guns go off so hard it shakes the china in my cabinet.

Once last summer a large drone from the base flew over my house. Several times. Practice maneuvers. I'm not sure how I knew it was a drone, but I did. It was quiet. I didn't like how that felt to me. It felt like when you see buzzards floating in the sky above your head.

I'm here to witness how quickly things can change. I'm from a place where people used to work and live and have lives of beauty and contentment for a while. We're not the only place on the planet in this condition.

My husband was retirement age when the layoffs started. Three of our children left. They moved out west. I encouraged this. My husband died two years after the shutdown. Cancer of course. I knew people would leave after the shutdown. I knew that some would stay. I thought it would be like when you wash dried beans in a colander and the little rocks are left behind, sticking to the metal. I would be one of the little rocks. The wheat or the chaff, I didn't kow. I imagined it would be old people who would stay. But young ones stayed. That's the deepest tragedy of it. They couldn't imagine another place, another life. There was disability for some of them, unemployment, old relatives to live with, invisibility on their side. Inertia. Sleepwalking.

The son who lives with me is named Jason. There's nothing for him here.

Imagine, if you can, a plague of dolls.

One day you're pulling weeds and you see the first one. Her neck seems to be missing some essential cartilage, the head not fastened tightly enough to the denim body. Some child made designs on her arm with marker, and her hair is ratty yarn. Someone has stuck pins in her arms, but she walks on thin legs and vinyl shoes, down the middle of your street. She had come from the direction of the old factory.

Oh, when I saw the first doll, I wanted to take her in! She looked like someone I had known, like someone's child. She stumbled in front of my house and looked at me. There seemed to be nothing behind the eyes. Who are you, you beautiful beautiful girl? The pupils were like sewn-on buttons. I wanted to run a brush through her ratty hair, but it was the kind of hair that would pull out in clumps. You would have to work your fingers through it to make any kind of sense of it. She lurched. I had never seen a doll walk like that without a child holding it. Was she some kind of drone as well? I looked for a child holding a remote control, but I didn't see one.

The doll turned away from me. She went into a house that used to shelter a family I once knew. For a while nobody lived there. Now somebody lives there. It's the house with the mattress on the porch. It meant something to the doll, that mattress. She looked at it good and hard. Someone inside would take care of her, she must have assumed. There was fabric covering the windows, though you wouldn't have called them curtains. Just fabric, or a sheet. I had gardening gloves on, and my knees were stained green.

I saw the second doll a few days later. This one was taller, more like a life-size fashion doll. She too came from the direction of the factory.

My daughter had a Barbie once that she let go very bad. The hair was like a fright wig. She carried it around by the legs, and let it play in the sandbox. The Barbie's hair was rooted, and she washed it with dish soap and plaited and combed and cut it, but then it stuck out all dry, no longer silky. So she colored the hair with Jell-O so it was a washed-out pinkish blond. She loved that doll for a while, though when she was older she found it in an old box of toys and took the head off and placed it on the Barbie's hand and took it to high school for Halloween.

That's what this second walking doll looked like, like the Barbie before she was beheaded; her head was on the neck stem. The head was tilted, but the hair was the same. She walked in that way you try to walk when you're young and you want to look sexy but you're really drunk.

This doll looked straight ahead. She was dressed in cut-off shorts and a T-shirt. Sandals. Her feet had not been molded into the shape for plastic high heels, the ones that always got lost so the doll always looked like it was pointing at something with her feet. This breathing (at least I think she was breathing) doll did not look like that.

The doll went into the same house, the one with the mattress on the porch. The fabric over the window was now red, though, or maybe there were two layers of fabric, to black out any light or to keep anyone from looking in. I imagined the two dolls in there together, perhaps with other dolls, a child's tea party. They would be bent at the waist, the tall doll with her long legs sitting up against the wall and the raggedy doll slumping forward and then jerking back up. They didn't seem like they belonged together.

Why do I always want to hold dolls when I see them? I often wonder. I want to protect them, to rock and sing to them. I love their sweet faces and the way the vinyl smells sometimes like talcum powder. There was a time when my children were old enough to have their own children but didn't. When I first entered the grandmother demographic, my daughter mentioned I looked at babies in strollers like I wanted to eat them. It was real hunger. I could bite into their soft sweet arms like an apple. Witch stories began to make sense to me, and fairy tales with wolves. I wanted them inside my belly. I wanted to hold them, rock them, love them to death.

But that was a year or two ago. It had been awhile since I'd seen any babies here. Just neighbors dressed in sheets and heading for the army base for their occasional bit of work.

So imagine my surprise when I heard what I thought was a baby crying at my next-door neighbor's. The neighbor is a young woman, early twenties. Her name is Delia. Her parents used to own the house. She came out on her front porch and beckoned me inside. Her eyes were blue and glassy, my neighbor's eyes.

The baby's name is June, she said. I didn't know you were pregnant, I said.

Neither did I, she said, but apparently I was!

I could hear the hiss of a vaporizer when I went into the house, the smell of baby oil and talc and burned coffee. Shh, Delia whispered. She took me into the spare bedroom. It was Delia's nursery when she was a child, and later her playroom. It was still done up as a nursery, with a crib and clouds painted on a blue wall, and a changing table and lace curtains. The crib had a blue lining with old tarnished lace spilling over the top, like a casket.

I looked down and saw the most beautiful sleeping child. It was lying on its stomach. She had beautifully messy light brown curls. Its cheek was pink, its hands curled into soft fists.

I watched that baby, waiting for it to move. It didn't move.

I'd love to hold her when she's awake, I said. She sleeps so soundly.

It's ok, she said, and she picked the baby up out of the crib and placed her in my arms. I could feel my breasts tingle. All these years passed, and the milk ducts have some phantom memory. June was soft and sweet and cool.

I made her, Delia whispered.

I had friends who'd done this. They bought the limbs and faces and eyelashes and eyes and body and fake tears and weights from a manufacturer. They used drill bits for the nostrils. They took off the factory paint and gave it a blue wash and then put on layers and layers of skin-toned paint.

Delia pointed to the child's cheeks. I used my own make-up, she said. She had weighted the dear sweet cloth body with pellets and she spent days attaching the hair. She told me something to that effect. She was going to make more and sell them on the internet.

Delia's hands were shaking. I put June back in her bed and went with Delia to the kitchen. I looked around. She hadn't washed dishes in weeks; bits of ketchup stuck on plates were scattered around the kitchen. No sign of any other food.

So this is what you've been doing with your time, I said.

The doll's skin feels too much like real skin, I said.

I suppose, she said.

And the eyes? I wanted to ask. Did the glass crack when you put them in? There was a kind of cataract-like haze to the eyes.

But I didn't want to insult her newly made baby.

Have you been eating, Delia?

She looked thin to me, wild-eyed and tear stained.

She pointed to the plates as though to say *of course*.

It was the time of year that ants busted open the peony blossoms and then came into the house, and there were ants running around the kitchen. They ran for the shelter of plate rims when you got near them. For the past few years, I've noticed, ants have taken on the sly habits of roaches.

I backed out of the house, turned and went down the front porch steps.

For the next few days June developed the unfortunate habit of crying in the middle of the night. The cry sounded mechanical, like something from a television set.

Delia was once my son's girlfriend.

After a day or two the girlfriend came out of the house dressed in a sheet and head scarf. She got into her car and headed to the army base. I hope she wasn't tortured.

If only the veneer mill were still open, she would have a regular source of income! The sweet smell of sawdust. A husband, my dear son Jason, to come home to every night.

She had left June in the house alone. I tried to get my son out of his bed, to come next door with me to see. Oh please please please, I said. He had been out late the night before, like every night. I tried to make him eat. He pretended to eat. He was always tired. His hair was blond. At one time I thought he might become a musician. I still hoped that for him. He was our pride and joy, our Jason. Our sweet angel baby. He helped his father through his final illness and he was so kind, so very sweet and kind. All the while we were telling him to flee. Don't stay here! we said. The painkillers came through the mail during the final illness, through all the final illnesses. Of course that's when it all started.

I went in the house and took the infant out of the crib, to the front porch where I could rock her. I wanted to warm up some formula and test the temperature on my wrist, but June didn't seem to require any nourishment. Perhaps she was made of watch parts. I loved her more than I should.

By this time in my story, the dolls were increasing. We found the infant dolls in dumpsters and the adult-sized dolls walking down the street at all times of the day. At one time there were at least fifteen hard-used fashion dolls with cut-off denim shorts within my one block alone. Men from the army base and from other towns had started coming to see the dolls. Wake up Jason! Get out of bed son, and do something!

The men pulled their cars into the alleys and the dolls bent at their bent place on their waists and leaned into the car windows. The men went with them into the abandoned houses. I'm afraid that money changed hands. The economy required an influx of these men, boys really. I started finding needles in my yard. The tips of the needles, it seems, were shiny with virus. Three of my children left the place. They live far away from here. My son, my beloved youngest boy, is now as thin as his girlfriend.

Under a microscope, a virus is beautiful. A greenish ball all pocked with dimples like an orange. Red pins on the surface and swirls of something painted on the ball. The swirls look like m's or like threes, something cursive and beautiful. It could not be random. Or like a peony made of copper wire, stamens of green that look like huddling fetuses. Influenza is like a blue and brown headed crib. You could lay down inside it and rest. Smallpox is hideous, as is dengue fever. But there are those that look like fireworks, like blue dandelions gone to seed, like deep-sea creatures. These are the ones that live here. So what if they're beautiful? Do you want to take photos of them?

If only we could have kept manufacturing all that sweet veneer. If only there were some hope for the children here. If only the farms were what they seemed to be when you drive past them in the fall and see the rolled hay turning silver in the evening sun.

We buried June right next to my husband in the churchyard. There was something not quite right with her from the beginning. My son is next to her now. Delia is still holding on for dear life.

Keep flying above us in your planes! From one coast to the other, keep right on flying over us! We test your bombs and your beloved warriors. Here. Right here. Look down.

Shock and Awe

When I was very young, my great-uncle took me and my brother to see the tomato slaughterhouse. I still remember the explosion of red fruit falling from a truck into sorting tubes before disappearing into washtubs and then reappearing on conveyor belts inside the windowless building.

Where they moved beneath a chartreuse light. A rain came down on the tomatoes then and a luscious juice of seeds and pale green and reddish orange liquid fell onto the concrete floor. This first rain was followed by another.

My uncle thrust his hand under a waterfall of tomatoes and then wheeled his chair over to where my brother and I were watching, one perfect skinned red fruit tomato in his hand. It was lye and skin raining down on the concrete, he told us, and I felt my throat close up in terror at the sweet juice I'd been imagining.

The round meat of the tomato lay in my uncle's hand like a heart, like throbbing sunlight, and he slid it into my hand where it felt alive and warm and much heavier than I expected. I passed the red to my brother. My uncle seemed proud of it, as though he had made the globe of fruit.

This is where our great-uncle had worked when he came home from the war. Before the war, he had been a farmer. After the war, he worked the line. Empty clinking silver cans. It was a lovely sound, like church bells or wind chimes. The cans were high above the tomatoes, high up in the eaves but moving down toward us in roller coaster chutes. The cans twirled and paused and dove in constant motion. They swooped down from the skies and in a short time swallowed all the fruit.

I remember my mother, our uncle said, in early fall ladling tomatoes into glass jars. It wore her out, he said. She seemed so pleased when I brought her home a case of these. Farming, he said, was never easy. But when I die, he said, would you scatter my ashes in the army camp where your father and I grew up? You won't be able to get close to the farm, he said, but our mother is buried there.

Years later, my brother and I launched our canoe in the Muscatatuck, several miles east of the army base. The river is one of those opaque olive-colored rivers, in places the color of old dollar bills. But there were silvery fragments of light on the surface that day, and all around a fresh green world, some of it reflected on the edge of the water as though it were paint, so you could look both up and down into the trees. It was late spring. I cradled the urn of our uncle's ashes.

We had graduated from high school the week before. We had no immediate prospects.

The inside of the canoe collected seedpods as soon as we were on the river: redbud, linden, cottonwood. It's like we were in a basket for seeds, every seed with a different type of locomotion. Why didn't they just walk, the trees? I asked my brother. I knew he was looking at the back of my head like I was crazy. So much effort to make all these seeds, and only some of them will take. I imagined the trees walking in the woods and planting each of its seeds carefully in a little seed bed, guarding it from predators, bending down over the little seedlings at night. Instead they just exploded at their given time while they stayed where they were. It was, I supposed, one way of living.

I kept stripping the tiny seeds off the threads of the linden and crushing them between my fingers, stripping the blades from the redbud beans and tossing them, blowing cottonwood seeds off my hand and watching them float on down the river. What else was there to do? I felt like I was cradled in a milk-weed pod, or something made of reeds, floating down a canal, like I was a baby myself, like we could start all over. Could we? I mean the world was alive and making copies of itself. In the first hour I saw a baby deer and a small red fox, and we passed a flock of newborn lambs.

There were no hazards in the river, no dips or rocks. Actually, it wasn't really a river at that point. More like a stream, maybe an irrigation ditch. We used the oars occasionally to keep away from shore, but for the most part we just floated. Water and sky and seeds and animal eyes and in the back of the canoe my twin brother, plotting our course. He laughed at things I said, but I knew that at some level he was imagining himself in some other adventure. The future didn't seem to demand any decisions from him. We were twins, but not alike.

We had a case of beer in the canoe, some water, a few cheese sandwiches. A cell phone in a baggie. My brother had stashed a duffle behind his seat. We rode low in the water.

We dozed and drifted. Drifted and dozed. I felt like a flower girl, blowing seeds along the way. When we reached the base, we were going to scatter the ashes then continue through the camp and portage the canoe up to the state road.

Our great-uncle and our grandfather had grown up on the base before it was a base. Their parents were sharecroppers. In the 1940s they had ten days to pack their stuff and leave before the army came and opened camp. Our army. They were in such a hurry, our father had told us. The soldiers blew up houses and churches and cords of cherry wood and orchards and anything else in their way. They brought in tanks and artillery and thousands of soldiers who were trained to fly. And just like that our great-uncle and his brother went off to war and the women and children and the aged moved to town and the women took temporary jobs at the mill and a whole way of life was gone.

I always say that my brother and I are not identical. It's a joke we have, but you'd be surprised at how few people laugh. He's six feet tall, and I'm five foot one. Inside we may be more alike. I don't know. Twins run in our family. Our grandfather and great-uncle *were* identical for a while, until one of them lost a lung in the war and one of them lost two legs.

The one who lost a lung wheezed and breathed hard whenever he tried to talk. Our father had picked up the sound of a one-lunged man from his father. Our mother pointed out to him that he didn't have to talk so softly. Still, our father talked that way until he died.

Our great-uncle lived in a wheelchair. He worked in a wheelchair. Sometimes he would let us take it for a spin. He had two replacement legs to attach to his knee stubs when he wanted to wear long pants to church or a funeral. This was two, maybe three or four wars ago, before legless soldiers came back with the metal hooked or bladed legs that allowed them to run like something prehistoric, some mix of bird and human. I wish he'd lived long enough to see that or to wear them. I would have loved to see him bounding through town.

It was the middle of the afternoon when I noticed something different about the riverbank. We'd spent four or five hours by then looking up through the leaves, and most of the leaves had been, I'm not sure how to explain this except to say that they'd been clean. Recently hatched and glossy. About three hours in, they started to look dusty. How close are we? I asked my brother. I was hoping he saw the same things I was seeing. Some of the leaves were curled, dry and black. After a bit there were fewer of them, and the land beyond the treeline was mostly new growth weeds, and instead of pollen coating the canoe, there was a layer of gray dust. My eyes started stinging and the air turned brown and all of the sudden it sounded like we had front row seats for the finale of a fireworks show. The ground itself was moaning.

Of course we were used to the sound of explosions from the base. We'd grown up with the sound. Sometimes it sounded like crackling fire and sometimes just low booms. When the cloud cover was low, the sound was magnified. We had heard the rumbling while we floated, white noise to us, but we had never been this close to the source. We're in, my brother said.

Along the state road there were warning signs when you approached the camp and tall fences with razor wire. There was a buffer of old growth forest surrounding the acres and acres of army things, and only one way in off the highway. Civilians could drive past a guard and go to a small museum that had old WWII bombers out in front. But that was as far as you could go unless you had one of the occasional part-time jobs where you'd pretend to be the enemy for an afternoon. On those days civilians were taken down dusty roads on school buses, all dressed in scarves and sheets and they would be set up in fake villages while army men captured them. That had been my own plan for scattering the ashes. I would do it subtly, dressed in a bedsheet. I had imagined carrying the vase up the outside staircase of a fake clay hut. I would trip and break the vase and the ashes would fall to the ground.

But my brother preferred stealth. He was sure he could get us closer to where the farm had been, and he was afraid that in my plan the ashes would be confiscated.

When we played army in grade school, the boys would capture the girls and put them in the play gym, and there was either a sexual thrill to that or sex, when it came, always had that same kind of thrill for me. Maybe that's why I'd gone along with his plan finally. At some level I imagined young men playing soldiers, chasing me while I opened the urn and let the ashes fly. I would let them capture me, but there would be no real danger since we were on the same side.

From the highway you could see the lines of barracks and pole barns and soldiers on break talking on their cell phones, and rows of tanks and cars but almost everything beyond that— the middle of the camp, the source of the noise—was hidden. I had no idea it would be this loud though, that the place itself would scare me.

Let's get this done, I said. Shh, my brother said.

I think this is a suicide mission, I said. Let's scatter the ashes now.

And what would we do then? he asked.

I thought there'd be wire delineating where the military world began. And in fact there had been, he said. Fences down to the river but not across. It's not like this is Los Alamos, he said. It's not like it's Fort Knox. Anything they did could be seen from satellite, he said. No spy would really bother to look here and no government would ultimately care if the place were lost. The wire fences were to keep civilians out while the soldiers played their games with real bullets. The camp was pocked and dry and dusty. Like the moon or Mars. Still.

Stop, I said. Right now. We can still get outside the base.

We're going to paddle on through, he said. There's no way out but through. The farm was in the middle, he said. We'll scatter the ashes there and then keep on going until we reach the other side.

This isn't Disney World, I said. This isn't Pirates of the Caribbean. This isn't It's a Small World.

When I'd been looking at the green world, he'd been steering the canoe into the middle of a war zone. If I'd been paying more attention to him, I might have known that was his plan. Because when I turned around to look at him I noticed for the first time that he was wearing his camo pants, that he'd thrown a camo shirt over his white T-shirt when I wasn't watching. And he wore a camo hat. It wasn't the kind of camo that you get in hunting supply stores—that old-fashioned kind that looks hand drawn. This was some kind of digital fractal print with a light green that seemed to recede and darker patches the color of shadows and bark and dark soils that advanced, so that the brother I knew seemed to disappear when I looked at him. If I looked at him against the canoe and stream, he looked like canoe and stream and if I looked at him against dead tree, like dead tree and against weeds, like weeds. I reached back in the canoe and touched the place I knew he was sitting, and I felt something like bone and flesh underneath the uniform. It was knee. He had painted his face.

I am not, I told him, quite ready yet to die.

His eyes were the only thing that still looked like my brother. Even then, I'd never noticed the hazel-ness of them.

Put this over you, he said, and he handed me a camo-patterned blanket. I saw myself disappear underneath it. He handed me some face paint, but I shook my head and dove inside the cloak. I kept a space open for my own hazel eyes. I told myself we were nothing but a log floating down the river now.

Right up the bank there were flat cutouts of men with springs on the back of them. A row of them standing in a line.

Further in the field a line of people dressed like my brother, the guns pointed at the cutout men.

The guns fired, less loud than I had imagined, or perhaps the sound couldn't hold its own amidst the booms of heavier artillery. However it was, the cutouts fell backward and popped up then fell again, like cartoon death. They couldn't shoot back, these figures. They kept falling and springing up and being shot again. On the front, they were made to look like people. On the back they were colorless. There were painted men with crossbody rifles, painted women in headscarves. There were children. I suppose there had to be children. It was like a shooting gallery at a carnival. We floated by. Some bullets missed their targets. Several came too close to the canoe. We're dead, I said to my brother. We'll be fine, my brother said. He seem quite convinced we would get out alive. And then? I asked. What will we do tomorrow and the day after that and the weeks and months and years ahead of us. That emptiness was the thing I really feared.

That's when I felt my feelings toggle, felt something like a thrill. I couldn't die, I thought. Because I hadn't yet died. But this is what it might be like. Now. Then now. We kept drifting. Around a hill and there were snipers shooting ground targets. They were high up in metal scaffolding. These soldiers were pointing away from us. The wind blew the snipers' hair. We were so close we could call to them. I wanted to call to them but was afraid of their reflexes. I began to feel invincible in my cloak of invisibility, in my camouflage, my green canoe.

When I close my eyes tight and press on them with my fingers, I see black with an explosion of white hot sun, but within seconds it goes away and all I see is flashing green like those night vision photos of bombing, and I imagine that thrill of the pitch-black nothingness turning into an eerie green some-thingness. In science class one year we made infrared glasses out of blue and red cellophane and for an entire weekend my brother and I walked around looking at the white blazing fire coming up off all the trees, telling ourselves in amazement that instead of seeing what wasn't there we were seeing what was really there, all the fire the green blocked out. And I imagined living in the universe the way it really was and not as it appeared to be. That red fox I had seen waiting to eat the lambs, coyotes with their own agenda. I imagined wearing night vision goggles on a battlefield, wildlife lighting up in the woods, the heat of life, all that same chartreuse glowing around me, the approaching wings of Jesus, the pop of white light from the thing I'm holding in my hand, the mystery of one thing becoming another. That would be my future.

By then I had forgotten the ashes. They were scarcely real. The flesh of the body, the blood and viscous eyes, the muscle. That's all that mattered. The fruit, the scattering of seeds. My brother grabbed the box from me and let the wind take the ashes where we thought the farm had been. It was a blown-up ghost town now, the farm. If I had the right lenses, I could see it. When we started to reach the other edge of the camp, it was almost dark. Oh brother, I thought, why did you bring me to this place? I can't go back. I wanted it more than anything I'd ever wanted.

Later, when he tried to explain to our mother what had happened to me, he would take out his box of plastic army men from childhood. Each one molded into its one posture, the way he'd placed them in rows and knocked them down. It was just play, he said. Like that! he might say. But in the middle of it all my sister crawling up the riverbank in her camouflage. I suppose he might be crying as he tells her this. I saw her making her way across a field pocked with ordinance, exploded and not, he would say. The way she seemed to crawl like a lizard or some shield-backed insect, in the dark. She disappeared until something swooped down from the eaves and took her away in its metal wings. That is, I know, when he lost sight of me. He couldn't have followed or even quite explained it. There was nothing he could do then. We were twins, but we had never been the same.

Transfiguration

HE ALWAYS HAD TROUBLE WITH HIS EYES. As a child, following behind the plow, there were times the sunlight would blind him. His eyes would tear up and close involuntarily, his eyelids turn red, and he would continue the row putting all his trust in the mule. He was nearsighted and that grew worse with the years. He was constantly being caught off guard by the shapes of shadows, seeing things he knew weren't there the way you can see things in a cloudbank. He'd be startled by a face in a stand of grasses, say, so he spent a lot of time talking to himself. Not an Aztec mask! he would tell himself. Not an angel! Just a nest of brown shadows or a concentration of light. He was not color blind. He was not crazy. It was the sensitivity to light that most bothered him.

None of this was enough to keep him out of the Army, when it came to that. (Though later in life, when he became legally blind and the world looked like something viewed through thick wax paper, he continued to drive his car to church and the grocery. His wife would sit in the passenger seat of the car and serve as his eyes as they made their way from one place to another. She was afraid to drive and couldn't overcome that fear, but they lived outside of town, and he knew the roads by feel.)

By that time, the surgeons at the VA had chopped the cataracts from his eyes, treated the glaucoma, but could do nothing for the macular degeneration. The lenses on his useless glasses were by then so thick that they obscured his eyes at some angles and at others made them appear (he was told) as large and round as a bullfrog's or a tree knot.

But the eyes were a secondary affliction. By the time his eyes gave out, he had lived for decades with only one lung. The lung he was left with whistled, and the ribs were caved in over the place his lung had been. Several of the ribs had been removed along with the lung.

His twin brother had lived the same number of years with no legs. He would have given his brother his legs. His brother would have given him a lung. Either one would gladly serve as the place to harvest organs for the other's continued life or even contentment. Kidney, liver. Each one was truly welcome to the other's heart. They'd felt like one person.

They'd both had dreams where they were a kind of ghost or lesser image and one would walk into the other until they merged and all the cells clicked and locked together the way they were intended to be. Even their memories would merge into one story. Then the one could hear and see and run and breathe like a young man. In the dream they are glorious to behold: all lit up like an Advent candle, like Jesus on the mountaintop. If they hadn't split in the womb they would have been too beautiful for any one woman, the girls said to them before the war.

But about the mule.

The first day of high school the brother who would lose the lung and his sight walked the seven miles from Nineveh High School to the farm and said he wasn't going back to school. No one would convince him otherwise. He couldn't talk about it, couldn't explain it even to himself except that something inside him hardened against it. All the family could get from him when they asked is that all he wanted to do with his life was walk the rows behind that mule and work the farm. He would help the family purchase those meager acres. He couldn't be coaxed or bribed. He was over six foot tall and couldn't be carried to school. And so at that moment the brothers who had always been together were separated during school hours. There was some conjecture that they took turns going to Nineveh, that both of them cut their hours to half time, that both of them were half scholar and half farmer, but it wasn't true.

For the next two years every day in the world one brother went to school and one worked the farm. The farmer twin plowed and planted, harvested alongside his father. The twins looked like the father—tall and dark. The boy also worked his mother's kitchen garden, helped her put up jars of tomatoes and beans. He helped her work a quilt. In the winter he helped his father cut wood and kept the fires going. He fed the chickens and snapped a neck for the stew pot on Sunday mornings. He hunted squirrel and deer and rabbit. He grew some ginseng for a cash crop, hired himself out to the sawmill when they needed hands, kept a small still and used their mother's canning jars for the potato spirits the boys would drink on Saturday nights at an old abandoned shack deep in the woods by the Muscatatuck.

One more thing: At the time he lived in the area, there was really no edge to it, nothing that defined it as a particular place. It was just *here* or *home* or *home place*. There were property lines and fences and county lines and hills too steep to farm and flat places that were made for it, but nothing that clearly marked this number of acres from any other until the army came and drew a line around those acres and those families within the line had ten days to leave and those families outside the area stayed. The absence of their ties from that point on pointed out the former presence. *Home.*

There had been a town called Kansas, Indiana. There was one churchhouse in Kansas, a one-room primary school, the preacher's house, a graveyard and a sawmill. Spreading out from Kansas there were three other schools, three other churches, fifteen cemeteries, two other sawmills, one other town (Pisgah) and within the area that would become the army training camp the descendants of six-hundred farm families that were deeded the land in the 1800s or were sharecroppers working toward the purchase of a few acres, like the twins' family. No one really made a distinction between the owners and the sharecroppers. The roads and hills had names. Drybread Hill, Crackaway Road, Ohio Ridge. The closest town that still remains with a store and a high school and butcher and bait shop was and still is Nineveh to the west and if you go further east and south, Edinburgh, where there used to be a veneer plant and lately there's been a plague of dolls.

You probably know that Nineveh is the town Jonah was running from when God stopped him under an eggplant tree and told him to go back to warn them about an army that was about to wipe them out. Jonah's refusal was the reason he was swallowed by a whale. This is a different Nineveh. Nineveh spelled backwards is 'Heven in.' Things like this occur to you as you plow, and they occurred to the brother who wanted to farm.

Kansas is the town listed on the twins' birth certificates. There are a few blurred pictures of Kansas in the library. I say this because when the army came, Kansas was blown off the face of the earth. The church was blown up, an orchard was blown up, lumber that couldn't be moved out fast enough was burned to ash. Most of the graves were moved. They had ten days to move before the soldiers came. Try looking up Kansas, Indiana on the internet and you won't come up with anything. That's how completely it was obliterated.

The Evening Republic.

March 5, 1942.Closing-Out Sale.

CLOSING OUT SALE

As we are all in the cantonment area we will sell on what is now known as the John A. Thompson farm which is now owned by Emerson Clark, 3½ miles west of Emerson, ... beginning on Tuesday March 10 at 10 a.m. (War Time):

6 horses, 10 Shorthorn cattle, 50 hogs (13 Duroc sows
and pigs; 3 Duroc sows in farros by date of sale; 25
Duroc feeding shoats; 8 pure bred gilts to farrow soon;
1 pure bred Duroc male hog) 265 bales of alfalfa hay,
extra good; 25 tons of mixed hay, baled; 5 tons of baled
clover hay; 800 bushels of good yellow corn in crib.
Farming implements: One international corn plant-
er with fertilizer and check row attachment; 3 farm
wagons, box bed ad combinations; three 1-row cul-
tivators; two 2-row Oliver cultivators; 2 McCor-
mick-Deerling mowing machines, one as good as
new; one 1941 used IHC power mower; one 1-horse
wheat drill; 2 walking 405 Oliver plows; 4 Oliver
14 inch sulky breaking plows; 1 spike-tooth harrow.

Lunch will be served by the Nineveh Christian Church

And so the sky grew dark with smoke from burning cherry
wood and burning churches, the wind blew soldiers in from the
coasts, the railroads brought in boots and uniforms and guns,
and barracks were built and the unsold hay was set on fire and
the wind blew and the wind blew and both boys helped their
parents load the wagon with quilts and sticks of furniture and
crockery and photographs of dead ancestors and baby shoes
and tiny baby gloves and old hat pins and the fruit of the previous summer's harvest, though some of it they had to leave
behind like they left the house that would serve as target practice for the soldiers before they went off to fight the Germans
and the Japs. They were told the land would be there for them

after the war. The Coes and Stillabowers and Nevilles and the boys would farm the land again after the fighting was done. No one understood that once the land is taken (as freely as it was in this case given) it is never returned.

The night before they were to leave the farm, the boys' father hung himself in the barn. His body was the last thing plowed under, quickly, with the help by then of other boys who were turning from boys into soldiers, their soft flesh hardening into something machine-like.

Of course the twins signed up. The one who would lose his legs went to the East Coast to train, and the one who would lose his lung was sent to Hawaii where he got TB. Had he not contracted TB he would have been sent to Bataan and would have lost, in all probability, much more than just a lung and I would never have been born.

But about the eyes. My father had never seen the ocean when he was sent out from the farm and hurtled toward it. He had never seen mountains. He had never seen deserts or been in a plane or a ship. He was more comfortable in the ship that took him from San Francisco to Hawaii than he was in the mountains because the ocean reminded him of the prairie.

It was too much, too quick. There was too much vivid color. A red cardinal in the middle of gray winter could clutch at his heart, but all the red in the world seemed concentrated in the jungle flowers in Hawaii, and all the green in the foliage and all the blue in the sky and in the ocean and all the light in the phosphorescent waves and in the sun's glare and molten rock that spewed into the air from the volcanos and he had never seen such stars.

In the cut-out place in the wet hot jungle his lungs began to fill with the bacillus. At first he thought the climate was the reason he couldn't breathe. It felt like his lungs were filling with steam. Like asthma. He didn't tell his sergeant, but he didn't need to. Soon there was the spit and wheeze and the sensation of drowning. All he wanted to do was to get back home and follow the mule, but the mule was gone and so was the plow. Who would take him?

Soon he was in an airplane drifting through the clouds, feeling so bad he didn't care if he died. And then they sent him to a sanitarium in San Francisco where he lay on a cot with white sheets and white curtains and there were white walls and he could hear the ocean and feel the earth's tremors.

He was in that room for seven years. Seven years while the war went on and the bombs fell and somewhere in Europe his brother lost his legs. In the sanitarium all the men turned pale and died and other men took their places. The nurses dressed in white and wore white caps and the news of the war came into the ward on white newsprint and some days the sclera of his eyes felt coated with acid. Everything was whitewashed to him, and the only vivid color was the red he coughed up daily. And the war went on and one day a girl came in with a dress made of a potato sack. She was a volunteer. And she came again and then again and every day he didn't die, though he thought he was going to. He thought she was a figment of his imagination until a few years later he married her. She would be my mother.

One day he woke up and one of his lungs was gone, his chest sunken, and his eyes saw what looked like wedding gowns hanging from the rafters.

He had been the one to find his father in the barn the day of the move. He'd pushed open the door and it was then he was sure there was something much different with his eyes. There was too much light! Pouring down from the sky through holes in the rooftree, the hay silver with light. The wedding gowns blew in the wind like sheets on the line, like cocoons being wound around something that was hidden, and then like ropes and then a single rope hanging from the rafter. He called for his brother, who ran on his then-good legs toward the barn and one of them held the father up and the other cut the rope and they placed him down on the ground and then the soldiers who had begun appearing outside the house began appearing in the barn and their mother came and saw what had happened. When the initial clamor died down, the boy who would lose his lung walked through the white light of the barn and untied the mule from his stall. What would they do with him in town, a mule that only served to pull a plow? We'll take him, a soldier said. You two help your mother. A few minutes later they heard a shot ring out in the woods. And so it began.

The
Town of
Whispering
Dolls

THE CONVENIENCE STORE IS LOCATED NEXT TO WHAT USED to be a Church of Christ on the bend in the road that connects The Town of Whispering Dolls to the lake in Nineveh. For a long while it was a convenient place to buy LISTERINE and NyQuil and SUDAFED and aluminum foil; to buy bologna, bread, and tampons, and squares of orange waxy cheese.

It proved convenient to have one gas pump in front of the store that supplied gasoline for lawn mowers and outboard motors and for cars. Inconveniently, the Church of Christ shut down several years ago. We watched the pastor die a long slow death that took him from a burly man to a bean before our eyes. But that's all history.

After a while the store added more candy and two-liter Coke bottles and energy drinks and powders that made the kids, according to reports, feel all jingley jangley in their muscles and their heads. It was a good feeling in a slow place and so it was the jingley jangley powders that kept the convenience store in business, I suppose, as they helped the sleepwalkers our children had become to surface partway from their sleep. And the bologna and the tampons were an essential part of the economy, as bologna never seems to go bad and it is not convenient for a girl to drive fifteen miles to the interstate when she starts to bleed.

As other things started to fall apart, most of us looked the other way as the shelves in the store grew more sparse and the headache remedies and bags of peanuts grew dusty and were separated by blank space like a museum of former convenience. I myself thought at the time it was inevitable, that eventually the shelves would go the way of the empty church pews, all the stuff and the store in which to buy the stuff oozing its way to someplace far away.

Still, for a while it remained convenient for the young people who lived in their parents' homes to gather there at night, sitting on the church steps or warped picnic benches, their skin yellow and blue in the bug and cell phone lights. The smell of black mold and other rot came through the broken door and the cracked windows of the church, from the cold basement and baptismal pool, a funereal odor that seemed to originate in the painting of the river on the wall behind the pool. At times it felt to me like it was the painted river that rushed into the dark night and transformed the children into what they had become.

And so the plague of dolls continued. Why are the dolls female? Dolls are almost always female because they are nurtured by females and we think being nurtured is a female thing.

It has always been convenient for me to think that, I suppose, because I had two sons and two daughters and not one of the sons wanted a doll and not one of the daughters wanted a male doll and it was only until the plague that boys from out of town started wanting to play with the female dolls.

I remember once when my son was a toddler and he took one of my daughter's naked rock-and-roll long-legged dolls and held it by the legs and beat it against the floor like the doll was a hammer. The doll's head stayed on, but it was skewed to one side when I retrieved it, and my daughter cried. We straightened the doll together, my daughter and me, and we combed its hair with a tiny pink hairbrush, and we dressed the doll in a denim skirt and fringed red shirt and cowboy boots, and we showed her younger brother how to treat it respectfully, and my daughter provided the voice when the now country-western rock star doll wanted to sing.

Still, it shouldn't have surprised me when the boys started to stay in bed until dark, a couple of them mixing the dark brews that I cannot keep my own son from drinking —the stink of it —sending the once beautiful dolls out in the daylight to bend at the waist and stick their heads inside of strange cars.

At one time I counted ten of these dolls in one afternoon, and I was always surprised when the heads came out of the cars still attached to the fragile neck stems of the bodies. Sometimes the dolls would get into the cars, their unbending knees causing them to lie flat out on the back seat or stick their legs outside the window or to lean back as though flinching from something. Sometimes the cars drove off and came back later, a human hand thrusting the dolls out onto the sidewalk.

They were badly used, these dolls, and I imagined them tangled together in some large toy box—arms, legs, heads and torsos intermingled. I wish that I could reach inside the box and disentangle them, to brush their hair as I did with my daughter's doll, to clean and repair them, to send them home in a cardboard box with plastic balloons from the doll hospital tied to their hands.

Back when my daughter was young, I do believe her Samantha doll came back from the doll hospital in Wisconsin with a different head. Its hair was that perfect. But that is ancient history. A sweeter time.

Oh beautiful children! Why did you have to grow?

One night I heard music coming from the church. Have you ever heard dolls whisper their prayers or sing? Their mouths don't move, but their voices are ethereal. A group of them had filled the baptismal pool with water and were soaking their pointed feet. Next door in the convenience store there were several dolls returned from playing at the army base. They were dressed in bedsheets and blankets, of course, and several of them carried their heads underneath their arms like motorcycle helmets. After a while it became the fashion to put the heads up along the shelves where the headache powders used to be and for the dolls to walk around town with the rounded neck stumps in the breeze. How lovely it must be to not catch sight of yourself in passing windows! How lovely to not be thirsty! Now and then when it seemed necessary to have a thought, the bodies retrieved their head or someone else's; that is, if the convenience store manager hadn't sold it accidentally or hidden it behind the counter for some fun.

And so, that's it about the convenience store, but what I want to tell you is that my potential daughter-in-law Delia was still alive and still hovering, it seemed, between the human and the not-so, if I may be so bold as to assume that I have not simply been hallucinating all of this.

I loved Delia, and more than anything in the world she wanted a child and I wanted to be the grandmother this would make me. Oh, how I wanted a soft baby to hold and teach to talk and sing and to find whatever beauty there was still left to find in this world! I mean I know the oceans are turning green with acid and eating into all the mollusks and snails and coral like a sugary drink eats into teeth or alcohol into the liver. I know this, I do, but I am still consumed by love for this world. I am consumed by love for trees, for instance, and for the sky when it's blue, and for flowers, particularly peonies and lilies, and as long as eyes can be thrown forward into the future to see them, I want them to be seen by a conscious being who can praise them. Oh how inconvenient my love is, perhaps how selfish.

And so after her daughter's death, when Delia came to me and said she thought she was about to make another child and would I take her to the doctor, my heart bled for her because of the disintegration of the town and community that would have sheltered her. We talked and cried over this. How would she support this child? Would it be healthy? There was a good chance that it would be born like June, if it were born at all, or that it would never take a breath at all, would be born with a bendable waist and rooted hair. And there was an equal chance that it would be born human like Delia herself had been born. The risk, how much could we take? Is it selfish to want your kind to persist, even if you're condemning them to death (as has always been the case when you think about it) or worse?

It wasn't clear to us. We had to drive to the city to see the doctor. It is a law in this particular state that women who see this particular doctor must watch a film then go home for the night and cry and then return the next day to this doctor if she has made one decision or make an appointment with a different doctor if she has decided to let the child marinate in what may or may not be toxic goo.

Delia and I settled into the dark viewing room to see the film. The first thing on the screen was a grainy photo of a man with arms like a butcher's. The man wears a butcher's apron. He pours what looks like liquid vinyl into three iron molds of baby heads. The vinyl is pink or brown or taupe. The molds are capped and then put in a furnace that spins the heads in a centrifuge until the vinyl coats the iron mold, we were told; the vinyl is heated so it sticks to the iron in the form of a head. When the molds are removed from the furnace the vinyl cools, the iron caps are then removed, and only the fontanels of the babies' skulls are showing.

The butcher writes the word *baby* with a Magic Marker on the top of every baby's head. Then he takes an ice pick and stabs the back of the sweet babies' heads to let out air. He sticks a gloved and oiled hand down into a mold and pops the baby's heated head out into his hand. He holds the baby's head out toward the camera and asks if we want to touch it. The head at that point looks so hot that it might burn the fingers. Behind him, on a shelf, there are rows and rows of babyheads and arms and legs. There are boxes marked *Jessica's right arm* or *Eric's left leg*.

The babies' heads at first have no eyes. Each one has a blank, Modigliani-shaped eyespace, or something like a space. In reality there are the eyelids and then an indentation for the football-shaped piece of vinyl that goes behind the eye. There's something Egyptian about the faces.

There's a hole in the back of the baby's head where the ice pick has gone in, and the man sticks an air hose in through the hole and then fills the head with air. The head blows up like a balloon or a cartoon head—the cheeks bulging, and the forehead, and finally the indentation where the eye would go, and a nurse takes round plastic eyes—the beautifully painted irises surrounded by half-spheres of white, like thick eggs over easy, and she places them on the bulging eyespaces and then removes the hose. As the air goes out of the head, the eyespace sucks the eyeballs into the head and suddenly the baby gazes adoringly at you and begins to cry. The camera zooms in to the fontanel, and you can see a regular quivering beneath the skin.

Even this small, the screen butcher says, it is alive. At this point, he says, we have a choice. I can remove the eyes and put the ice pick back in the now-beating place and put the pieces on this shelf behind me, or I can send it down the line where women will make them voile christening gowns with beautiful buttons, molded felt hats with ribbons, where another woman will paint the lips and apply blush and eyeshadow and another will affix the eyelashes and trim the lower ones and apply a wig over the holes in their heads using a glue gun. And another woman will stuff the torsos with cotton and tie the heads to the bodies and the arms and legs and the one who puts the final stitch in the back of the torso will number each child in the book of life, unique and absolutely irreplaceable until they break your heart or die of natural causes.

So what will it be? he asks.

And so we go home that night and weep and cry, but given the toxicity of Delia's uterus and blood, there is no other way than the way that she has chosen. The next morning we return to the doctor's office. It is the day he does surgeries, and there are men and women outside passing out pamphlets as we drive around to the back. Delia takes a handful of stuff a woman hands her through the window of the car. I am reminded of Delia's own head disappearing in the car windows. Delia throws the stuff the screaming woman gives her into the back seat of the car. As I park in back and get out of the car I notice that one thing she's been given is a tiny bean-shaped, plastic, unborn baby doll. How could they be so cruel?

We are buzzed into the locked building and inside women much like Delia, from many different places and each with their own problems, sit in waiting room chairs and tell each other their stories. While anesthesia is sometimes available, there is no nurse on call to deliver it and the price, even if there were a nurse, is prohibitive. That is fine, Delia says. I should feel it, she says. It is what I deserve. No, I say, you do not deserve this, I say. I know the pain she will be feeling. I can feel my own harvested uterus contract. It has remained a phantom limb.

After a few hours, Delia is taken to the surgical theater. She comes back out in a few minutes with no color in her face. All the blood has been suctioned from her, it seems. She is shaken and small and all the women in the waiting room hug each other because they're all they have in this world and all they will ever have.

There are no organs inside a doll. There is only air. When we get back to town, at her request, I drop Delia off at the convenience store where I hope that she can still purchase something for the pain.

The
Wind Farm
at Night

I'LL SAY THAT SOMETIMES THE CLICK OF THE TURBINES makes us crazy. All day the light and shadow strobing in the house. Every day the strobing burns itself more deeply into my eyes until I'm afraid the light will turn dark and never go away. How to explain?

You know how if you've been driving all day you can close your eyes when you get home and still see the country moving in front of you, only now it looks (the country) like an X-ray version of itself because it's behind your eyelids? Or how you can be out in bright sunshine and then come inside and what you thought was a light-filled house suddenly seems like a dark one? It's like that, except I'm afraid at some point my eyes won't adjust to light again.

It's not a complaint really. Really, it isn't. In the northern part of the state, up near Chicago, the ground is toxic, and my sister is raising her children, my nieces and nephews, there. I know it could be worse, is what I'm saying.

And they are lovely, the turbines, better than power lines, particularly when the sky is blue. Sometimes I do stare at them. The blades look like ballerina's legs, but all calves and no feet, like ballerina's legs but with the feet chopped off at the ankle, like a German fairy tale. I can picture all the feet with the toes balancing in satin slippers, waiting in a storeroom for the day they'll be reattached and all the blades will jump from their towers and start dancing. Judgement day! Would that be a sight to see!

At night sometimes my daughter walks through the wind farm and heads toward the factory. She doesn't see me following her. The factory name glows red at night. Up ahead, my daughter's black socks are soaked with dew. She's without shoes, of course, like the turbines, and she pulls her shawl closer. Some nights she has enough time to almost make it there, get back to the house, plug herself into the milk vein, hope she doesn't die this time, hope she might. Most nights I'm there to catch her when she falls.

The parking lot is pink with vapor lights in the distance, not as many cars as when we all worked there. The difference between the uneven fields and pavement makes my daughter's legs shake, her knees give way again. She lurches herself forward. Her hair is knotted. How long since she has combed it?

You know, when I was young and a fool, I ran away to New Mexico to see a boy who said he loved me, and I believed him. I left everything behind for him. He wrote songs and he said they were about me. It took me awhile to realize I was a vampire's girlfriend. There were so many times I should have seen this. He used my credit card to buy gifts for other women and stole a garnet ring I was given by my mother. He would never admit to the ring, but I had him dead to rights on the card and when he cried and begged and said he was no good, still I forgave and forgave him.

I loved it in New Mexico. At sunset the mountains turned red, and the aspen leaves shook. Sangre de Cristo, though the red never looked like blood to me because it was light. It was more like a wash of red or a sudden glow of what was always there, but you hadn't noticed it.

We lived out near Taos. He made songs out of my blood and the mountain's. It was nothing as dramatic as a cut, more like a slow transfusion of my life to his until one day when he was singing on the square and other women were looking at him, and the jealousy was making me weak, I realized I was a fool. I wasn't special. Why had I given him my body? I was food, and he would eat whatever was offered to him and soon I would be consumed.

My daughter never quite believes me when I say that I was pretty then. Ha! I know. And I could sing. All my life, I'd sung in choirs, second soprano or alto, so I could add harmony to anything. It's amazing how you can change the tone of something by ending with an open fifth chord, say, instead of a third so it sounds mysterious and medieval instead of sweet. When you really stick that open fifth and don't slide into it, when it comes at the end of a song it sounds like you believe the tone will go on forever.

In high school I thought I would be famous and never thought I'd end up living in the Midwest again. I came back home to my own parents, who have passed, but I wasn't as empty as I thought I was. I was carrying a child, my daughter. She is and has been the one true love of my life. I thought someone should know how I got her in case, like her stepfather and her boyfriend, she is taken away.

They used to sit on my front porch in the evenings, after their shift was done. The movement of her arms as she works is so beautiful, the boy told me. That's what he first noticed about her, he said. When she took off her work gloves, her fingertips were lacquered, unchipped. Red or black or midnight blue, metallic silver. Square shaped at the tips, like cars, he said.

I was retired by then, recently widowed. I brought them sandwiches on plastic plates most nights, sweet tea, then disappeared inside. My beautiful girl and this boy. I would help raise their children, and that would be my life. Bit by bit, in my imagination, I imagined the child. Green eyes and ginger hair and soft baby feet and wrinkled baby hands in fists, those sweet soft fingers and soft nails.

They looked so tired. They worked too hard, I told them. I tried to feed them more. I sent them to work with food, fed them when they came home. Fried chicken and potatoes, pie, dark beer. Still, they lost weight. Sometimes they wouldn't come home between one shift and another. I would see his pickup parked in town, the two of them looking half asleep in the cab. Like babies. I told myself they wanted their privacy.

It was hard, I'm sure, living with your girlfriend's mother and in her house. They were saving their money, they said, to rent their own place. One morning they didn't come home and I drove toward town in the early morning and saw his truck outside a house with tablecloths on the windows and rusted bed springs and engine parts in the yard instead of flowers. I'd gone to school with the woman who lived there. Her mouth looked like barbed wire, all black teeth and worry lines. And I'm afraid there are tangles in her brain like electric cords thrown helter-skelter in a plastic tub.

I knew what was going on but couldn't stop it from happening. I would think it was over and then it wasn't over and then I'd think it was over again. There were tears. There were promises. Over and over and over, just like it had been with her father. I'm one of those who always wants to believe and so I do it over and over even when I know I shouldn't. If I stopped believing, I don't think I could stand this world. I believe despite all the signs that tell me not to.

It would be all right, I thought. They had each other. They had work to go to. They had a plan. They had my love. They still believed their promises when they made them.

You would think an entire community couldn't live on candy, but ours did for years. The factory still makes candy, so much that you can hardly go into a drug or convenience store in the entire world without seeing bags of it. At one time or another we all worked there. We measured. We poured. We stirred the vats of gelatin and sugar. We filled the molds. We took the heated molds and put them in the cooler and we removed them. We dusted the candy with cornstarch. We separated the bags and watched each one fill and seal. We placed them in the boxes. We counted. We counted. We maintained and repaired the machinery. And while we did this, we talked to each other. We watched as our friends' children came to work there. We knew the stories of the founders, where the bosses lived. We raised our children on the seconds, filled their Christmas socks with distorted gummy candy. Sometimes the gummies would stick together into something resembling space aliens or superheroes, and the children would play with them as though they were.

A couple of years ago a big shipment of packing crates was delivered to the factory. The factory shut down for a few days as the old machinery was dismantled and sorted and put into the crates and hauled away. My daughter, the boy, everyone participated in the dismantling. Take this shovel and dig, I thought when they told me about the crates. They knew it too but they were still optimistic. They would be getting shiny new machines to work with, the healthiest machines. New break rooms, new molds, new lines of candy.

In a few days they saw their folly as truck after truck pulled in and unloaded boxes of machinery that looked so strangely human. Like a perfected skeleton of a person but without the flesh. A cheerful yellow they were, the yellow of a caution light, all smooth curving tubes for arms and hands. Without reproductive or digestive systems, without heads. The center of gravity was down by the wheels so they could lean in so very gently over the candy, picking up the trays and sorting, indefatigable. Ingenious. Why weren't we built like that? A few mechanics could run the factory after that, and they would dress in white coats like doctors. The rest of us were unnecessary. What do we do now while we're waiting for our marching orders? What do we do next with our lives?

My daughter and her boyfriend were laid off, spent more time at the dark house in town. It wasn't long until the boy fell asleep in the truck and she couldn't rouse him. It was early in the epidemic. Nighttime, now, her pupils jet buttons. I know what to do to save her but it takes constant vigilance. I can't fix her but I can try to save her.

I just need to walk it off, she says one night. All will be well. And so she walks out the front door, trips, slides down the front step as though she has no bones. She stands back up, her legs noodley, walks through the wet black fields underneath the turbines, toward her new lover.

She is not well. It's breaking my heart. Now she gets the shakes, she's always cold, her teeth hurt and her fingernails ache, she tells me. But something in her, some nights, pushes her toward him. It's an old story. How long will it take her to realize he'll never really see her?

They're beautiful really, she told me once. She was delirious. For a while, she says, I thought I had a crush on one of them. I would look through a window into the factory, she said, and watch it. Him, she said. He seemed different. I imagined the arm reaching out to me, she said. Sometimes, she said, I fantasize about that, lying on the table and passing by him, him knowing exactly what to do with me.

You're delirious, I said to her, but she didn't hear me.

At night there are only a few blades turning slowly. So quiet, the hum. The power has been collected, is going somewhere, though I'm not sure where. Does anyone know? Is it Chicago? And the money, do we know where that is going?

I follow her those nights when she tries to reach him, and

I catch her when she falls. I'm not sure she even knows it's me who's carrying her. She's so light in my arms. She's always dreaming.

All the fields were sold off over years. Over time, most of the young ones moved away or are now in the process of dying. The ones who stayed did so out of duty, or out of fear, or even out of love for the place itself. Sometimes I feel like I'm standing on a small island with the shoreline eroding away all around me until someday it will be just the house and my daughter and I will be standing on the roof and then it too will sink and we'll both go under.

But when the corn and beans are combined, and the dust and chemicals are stirred up in this flat country, the sunsets in this place are also glorious. Such purples and oranges and pinks and at night the stars! I can still see her. Green eyes and ginger hair. Soft baby hands and nails. Soft baby feet. Behind my eyelids, still, I'm assembling their child.

Game Night

Needles

THERE'S THE NEEDLE YOU STICK IN THE DEFLATED basketball before attaching the air pump, the needles on the white
pine that fall one day in autumn and turn red on the ground,
there's the different thickness of needles in a sewing kit. There
are wood and plastic knitting needles and metal knitting needles the color of popcorn bowls and metal cups (like the blues
and greens of bicycles with their black-and-white tires and the
needles you use to inflate the tires) and there's the particular thin needle your mother used to stitch the sleeve of your
brother's best suit before he was laid in the casket. And there's
the needle the undertaker used to sew his lips shut.

There are the needles you set in the groove on vinyl re-
cords to release the sound, there are needles that measure the
sound, and acupuncture needles, and trussing needles for tying
the legs of poultry before it's cooked and then there are the
slim silver needles, fine as broomstraw, that pierce human skin

and flesh and the elastic tubes that carry blood toward the heart. You will need several of the latter. Or you can share one with your neighbors. Do not make this second choice.

Syringe

IN SOME STATES YOU CAN FIND THEM AT THE DRUGSTORE. In other states you can't. Don't look for any logic or consistency. Don't look for kindness. The gamekeepers want to think the worst of you. You know that. In the states where you can't buy syringes easily, you may run into trouble. It will not stop your play, but the play will be more dangerous. In those states the game is more like gambling. Oddly enough, gambling itself is often legal in those states. As you know, our state is one of them. I am so very sorry for this because it means, unfortunately, that you will quickly join the dark side of the game. My dear, my dear one. The risks will be greater for you. It can't be helped.

To put all the risks out on the table, know too that this is a state where you cannot exchange your needles at the end of play, even if the milky drip of liquid and blood is still clinging to the tip of the one your teammate hands you. It seems to be the thinking that the needle itself is what drew you to the game.

And while it is true that sometimes just the sight of the needle or the prick of any needle will give you a fleeting temporary relief, it is not enough. So you will make your own arrangements. God save you as you roll the dice.

So when you cannot find needles easily, find a relative or neighbor who is diabetic. If the neighbor is elderly, he or she will think the syringe has been misplaced and will soon purchase others if the pharmacist will allow it. Pharmacists are drunk with power, and it may be difficult for the diabetic who pleads and whimpers. But don't think about that. Protect yourself.

If you still have a credit card, dear one, order your kit from eBay. Or go to a fisherman, as they have their own sources for rigs that they use to inject air beneath the skin of earthworms so the bait does not join the algaed muck at the bottom of a river or a lake. This is true. Buy some wading boots and a pole, or steal them from Gander Mountain. Listen to the recordings of birds. Peruse assault rifles like a good citizen. Move to fishing supplies. Fishermen are seldom questioned about their rigs. Diabetics, on the other hand, are sometimes treated like criminals.

And one more risk: if you are caught with any of this, you will end up in jail. Where, even if you're not sentenced, you might wait a year or two for a defense attorney to plead your case. Ultimately, this may be for the best. But you will never ever get a job should they appear again. This is all part of the game as it is currently played in the heart of the country. Dear one.

A Note on Water and Spoons

Do not be afraid to ask questions of your friends or family. Some compounds dissolve easy in room temperature water. Some dissolve only when heated. Heat is your friend, as boiling water may kill certain viruses. It is recommended that you boil all the water to begin with. Please. Do not become impatient and use cold dirty water or forget to bring the boiling water back down to room temperature. I regret that I must say these things that might seem obvious, but I must.

(When you were a baby, I was given a ceramic handled spoon at a baby shower and I fed your dear brother strained peaches and strained peas and used the soft side of the spoon to carefully make a second bite out of the food that oozed from the corners of his sweet sweet mouth. As you grew, you followed him everywhere.)

How to Play

SO YOU'VE FOUND A SYRINGE AND A SHORT NEEDLE, ultrafine if you can get it. Thick needles will work but make a popping sound that may frighten you. You've dissolved the compound and filled your kit.

If you can, find someone to do this with you as games are not meant to be played alone. Find several someones. Practice how you will call the hospital should one of you require it. Practice hiding your kit so you will not go to jail. Think of this as military training. You do not, under any circumstances, abandon your buddy. You would never jump into the stone quarry with no one with you. You might break your neck or drown unremarked upon. Tap into that old knowledge. And don't worry. If you live in certain hidden areas of this country, players will be plentiful. Just look around you and someone will appear.

Oh, there was a time when your game board was a small theme park of courthouse, Victorian homes and workers' cottages, veneer mills, gardens, churches, a hardware store and knit shop, children on bicycles, a Carnegie library, perhaps even an archive of local history, and a restaurant where old men and farmers gathered in the winter over thick white mugs of coffee. And at the edge of the game board, grain elevators filled with seed and the flatness of green fields that sounded and looked like the ocean when the wind blew across them. The sunset was as crimson on the western horizon as it was on the Gulf of Mexico. I'm here to tell you that the sunset is still as beautiful, but I know the game will keep you turned toward the center of the board.

So. First, choose and clean your site. With practice, you will become skilled at judging the direction and width of your chosen vein.

Use gravity to bring blood to your limb before applying your tourniquet. Swing or hang your arms, for instance. Make a fist. Try to secure rolling veins so they won't roll. The method of securing rolling veins varies from person to person, and you will become proficient with practice. Be sure not to leave the tourniquet on too long. As the blood's tubing rises to the surface of your arm, it is tempting to stop and watch and waver. Do not do this. Make a choice.

Make sure the needle bevel is opening face-up. Remember the goal is to quickly get the liquid to the heart.

The needle should be perpendicular to the injection site. I cannot overstate this. You must have confidence when you make the insertion. Think about the times you've had blood drawn, how the skilled phlebotomist dives into the vein like an Olympian and sticks the landing. Be that Olympian, and whatever you do do not be cautious as you insert the needle through the skin and muscle, probing for the vein's tubing. This will cause the vein to roll. So insert! Just do the stick.

When you think you're in a vein pull the plunger back to

see if blood swirls into the syringe. If the blood is dark red and slow, then in fact you've hit a vein.

At this point untie your tourniquet and inject. If you do not hit a vein despite following these directions, or if your arm turns numb or you notice it turning blue, untie your tourniquet, pull your needle out, and wait before you try again. Gather your courage. You may try several times at first. If you are not properly positioned in a vein when you push the plunger, you will be putting your drugs into the tissue surrounding the vein, or under the skin, or some mysterious black hole, dark matter. In addition, the tissue will be painful and will swell and the effect of your drugs will come too slowly. You risk an abscess. So be patient. Find the vein.

If you follow the rules, you will feel immediate relief. You may feel as though you are one with God. Rest assured that it is not God you are at one with. Still, if you'd like, pray to your god. Praise, gratitude, supplication, confession of sins. Each prayer will be appropriate. You will need all the help you can get to make your way into, through, and back. The goal of the game at this point will seem to you to be metamorphosis. But listen to me. The real goal, for you, is to stay alive until I can find a way to save you.

And so as the rush begins, don't forget the vein you've tapped. Carefully pull the needle out of the injection site at the angle it went in. Apply pressure to the site to stop the bleeding. Don't use alcohol pads on a fresh injection wound.

On the Choice of Partners

YOU WILL SIMPLY RECOGNIZE EACH OTHER. In the winter, you and the others will huddle in the only house in the neighborhood that currently has heat. Neighbors, your neighbors' children. Despite our best efforts, you came to the game at different times and as you know for different reasons. All the reasons go back to the fact that the game board has drastically changed. Know that it always does, though. War, drought, famine, illness, death, poverty. The game board changes underneath your feet. We did not want you to feel the pain of this.

In your case, instead of the verdant grid you carry in your memory and that I carry in mine, outside the blanket-covered windows the snow now covers shattered county roads, the abandoned mill, the abandoned casket factory, the abandoned storefronts, the now-industrial farms that no longer require the tending of plants or animals but of monstrous machinery. (At night the machines are lit with headlights, a man sitting in an air-conditioned cab listening to talk radio.) Do not stop to mourn the past! Remember your mother worked forty to sixty hours a week and when she felt her soul emptying she would go to church or drive up to the city or the outlet mall by the interstate and the two of us would buy resin mirrors made in China, silk flowers, a faux painting of wine bottles or coffee; a T-shirt in several colors the softness of kittens, the thickness of tissue paper, made of recycled pop bottles to soothe your conscience and to take your attention away from the fact that in the wash the T-shirts would develop tiny holes. We were assured that this is the trend, one which will require the purchase of several more T-shirts but in the meantime here is one with the tiny holes manufactured into the fabric from the start. Doesn't it look good? Is it not hip? Do you not want it? Are you not beautiful in it? Doesn't it soothe your soul?

The purchase of these things was a drug itself and at night you would look at the glittering colors of objects and for a while it would satisfy you until once again you felt yourself emptying and you would begin again.

So what has changed? In all the years you learned nothing from me other than the syringe that sucks in money and then releases it. So when the money comes from disability checks (how hard it was to get that documentation!) or from your discharge from the service or from selling your body at the convenience store, and you need desperately to play the game because it has become, as you can see, the only game, then what are you to do?

How could it be otherwise?

Dear one. Listen:

If you want to play, you must understand you've made a choice you will regret. Every day in the world you will tell yourself this is the last time you will succumb (the last dessert before the diet, the last purchase on a credit card, the last time you will sleep with him, the last lie you will tell, the last theft you will be forced to make, the last drink, the last injection, the last time the very last) and every morning you will wake in shame and the only thing that will ease the shame is more of the thing that caused it. I know this. I wish I had a well of wisdom to give you. I wish I had it now. You were so fragile. I loved you beyond reason. I wish I could have kept you in a sort of womb filled with beauty and light and angels. Sometimes I'm sorry I brought you to this world. Mea culpa. Mea culpa.

Forgive yourself. Religions were created to protect you from this process. They have always been this powerless.

Resurrection

WHEN THE LEAVES TURNED YELLOW AND THE COLD October rains began, children in the elementary school were given egg babies to care for. They spent recess making cribs out of shoeboxes, and some of the children made cunning little onesies out of cloth cut from the legs and arms of old clothes purchased from the five-cent box at yard sales.

Those who were interested in design (and there were several) put shoeboxes together to make a sort of house, often with backyards, and playground equipment made from spoons and straws smuggled in from the lunchroom. The most elaborate of these were displayed on the craft table to show the grandparents who showed up on Parents' Day.

Some of the children wrapped construction paper around the shoeboxes and drew on windows and doors and made dividers for the inside of the box. When the teacher said the box was supposed to be a crib, these children scoffed because the box was way too big for one baby and besides, the baby would never grow any larger. They made a smaller space inside one corner of the box for the baby and picked grass and then crunched leaves for the baby to sleep on. Then they made paper dolls or brought in little plastic or rag people the size of grown-ups' thumbs, usually toys from fast-food meals or discards from larger sets of army men or PLAYMOBIL or Fisher-Price. They put the little people in the boxes with the babies and said they were the mothers or fathers or brothers or sisters or cousins. There were no boyfriends or girlfriends or step anything because the children decided that adults would only be known by their blood relation to the baby.

During the day, the children would take the little people out of the box, leaving the babies alone in their mangers. They made the little people hop from desk to desk looking for something to do while the children were supposedly filling out worksheets, preparing for their futures. Sometimes a child would sneak a mother or a sister inside a desk with a plastic soldier or miniature man and they'd do what older people do in the dark. The man would leave after and maybe go into another desk and the mother or sister he left behind would come out with a dusty penny or piece of hard candy and then go back into the box with the baby and fall into a sleep so hard you had to shake them to wake them back up. It could have been a girl soldier with a father or brother of course, but that's not a scenario any of the children had seen. Usually the fathers and brothers died in cars or basements or wars and the mothers and sisters were left with the babies, though lately a lot of them had been dying too. Everyone, it seemed, waited for the grandparents and great-grandparents who, at least a few of them, could sometimes be counted on, if only to grieve.

The children were supposed to take the babies home with them each night. They had to walk home with the babies without dropping them on the street. Some of the babies didn't make it, and a child had to watch its baby's skull crack, the yellow brains ooze out. It was not a contest, but the children felt the one who kept its baby safe the longest would win nonetheless. One child lost so many babies at night and even during the day at recess that his desk was covered with death and birth certificates, because of course you couldn't have one child doing nothing in a classroom while the other children were caring for their babies. So the child's baby was given a funeral and a certificate of dying before being composted, and then the child was given a new one. Clumsy child, though. The new baby was usually gone before the day was out and a replacement brought from the refrigerator.

The compost heap was in the back of the playground near the wildflower garden, right next to the exhibit of native prairie grass. In early fall, explosions of stinging yellow jackets flew out of the ground by the compost, and the children adopted a zigzag pattern of running to get away from them. The teacher kept an EpiPen in her pocket, cocked and loaded, because she didn't want to move the graveyard away from the gardens. She'd read on Facebook that both compost and bees were good for flowers and she was a young enough teacher that she hoped to save the world. She added table scraps from the lunchroom and coffee grounds from the teacher's break room, and along with the dead babies, she was making some rich loam where before there had been nothing. Little wasps. Now fall was here and the workers were all dying off, leaving one fat satiated queen and these babies raising their own fragile babies and so on.

The babies had been the teacher's idea from the beginning. She learned it at college, so it wasn't an original idea in the larger world, just one new to this community. It had started years ago as a way to remind children, when the hormones started in a few years, what it meant to care for a baby. It's fragile! You can't get rid of it! Of course none of them remembered that lesson any more than they remembered their multiplication tables. She knew this because she'd been in school with some of their parents and now here they were, the offspring.

The fragile shells in the shoeboxes were porcelain and brown and spotted and some of them shades of aqua, but inside all of them was the same goo. Perhaps that was the real lesson.

Wouldn't it be easier if we boiled them, one of the children always asked her, as though he'd been the first one to ever think of it.

You could, she told the child, but then the baby would be dead, wouldn't it?

Oh yes, the children said, but we'd be off the hook. We could throw them to each other on the playground, have them sit next to us on the buses without worrying that if they fell on the floor and rolled away, they'd die. They might crack, of course, but inside they'd be all soft and sweet, like a puffball, ready to be born.

Not entirely, the teacher said, because the smell of rot would not be pleasant.

I would eat mine before it rotted, one of the children always said, and then the ones with active imaginations would turn to the child who said that and hiss *cannibal*.

One of the children said she realized you couldn't put the goo back inside when it came out, but she wanted to start a hospital for the slightly injured and the teacher said sure, why not. They decided to put the hospital underneath the stage in the cafetorium.

The child who ran the hospital had a mother who was a licensed practical nurse (LPN), so she had been around hospitals. She chose as her assistant a boy whose older brother had left the house in an ambulance, his body covered by canvas, even his face, so the boy knew about emergency vehicles. It was his job to run sick or cracked babies down to the cafetorium in the watch box that the teacher's Christmas present watch had come in.

When a baby's child thought she'd heard her baby crying like she was sick or hurt but didn't have any outward signs of cracks or pain, the doctor who ran the hospital would simply keep it for a day or two in a dark place and let the child come in to rock it at recess. The doctor knew that sometimes it was the child that needed the quiet dark space for just a while and not necessarily the baby who was ill. The doctor would get the child to talk about what was wrong with the baby and sometimes the stories of what the little people had done to the baby were so horrific that the doctor would think of closing down the hospital so she wouldn't hear the stories anymore. She was such a good doctor that sometimes a child would bring a little person who had stopped moving into the hospital, hoping for a miracle. He's dead isn't he? a child would ask, and the doctor would nod her head gravely and say she was afraid there was nothing she could do. They would cry together then and when the child was done crying he would go back to the classroom where another child would help him write an obituary. The teacher was pleased at how the children worked together and all the life skills they were learning.

Once or twice the doctor herself, or her assistant, would accidentally drop a baby and the teacher would sneak a replacement down to the hospital, and the baby's child would usually never know the difference. There was in fact only one hyper-observant child who had held her baby up to the light once and was able to identify the tiniest bit of gray transparency in one spot on the baby, and so wasn't fooled.

All of this went on through October. The first week in November the skies turned the leaden gray they would remain until April and the little people in the boxes went into a kind of funk. More and more of them began disappearing together into a shoebox owned by a child who was spending a few weeks with his father. The teacher always kept his desk just like it was when he left so there would be some consistency in the child's life when he returned. But when the owner was away, no one was taking care of the shoebox and it became a place with an unsavory reputation. The children told their teacher about it, and she asked the principal if a social worker might be persuaded to come to her classroom, but he reminded her that there were only two in the entire county and their plates were full. The only child temperamentally suited to take on a social worker's role was the doctor, so as was usually the case, the children did without one.

So the little people kept going into the abandoned shoe-box and some of them stumbled back to their own shoeboxes and some were covered with canvas and sent by watch box down to the hospital. When they didn't return, no one knows what happened to them except for the doctor and perhaps the teacher. They were too toxic to put in the compost heap. A couple of them were in the back of the hospital with IVs and breathing tubes made from the same lunchroom straws they used to make playground equipment. It was rumored that the rest were thrown in the trash.

No matter. The doctor's main concern was the babies, of course, keeping them alive. But some of the babies seemed to be showing signs of abrasions and if you looked at them long, the baby's child said, you could see them jerk like they were having seizures and inside their poor little hearts were beating irregularly and you could sometimes see the heartbeat through the fragile skin.

By the end of the first week in November, the doctor was overwhelmed and sad. She had permission to stay late after school and she sat underneath the stage listening to the AYS kids doing their homework and eating their snacks. It was all a distant sound, and it sounded a little bit like music to her as she sat in the semi-dark surrounded by babies. There were ten in the neonatal unit this week, lying there so still. She took the vital signs of each one, and there were, as far as she could tell, no vital signs, or only very faint ones. What would she tell her classmates? Her teacher couldn't keep supplying babies. Soon it would be the holidays and she would have other things to think about. And what purpose did it serve to keep replacing them? They would grow up to be the little people who hopped from desk to desk or spent the day sprawled out on the floor of the absent boy's shoebox.

The doctor's mother had sent her to school that day with a safety pin holding up the hem of the pants she was wearing. Her mother, the LPN, was not doing particularly well and the doctor was feeling a kind of despair she wasn't used to feeling. Most days she woke up feeling that she was a real doctor and she believed despite everything that someday she would be one or a teacher like her teacher. But some days, like today, she didn't know how she could make that happen.

She looked around her at the babies lying in the soft flannel nests she'd made from one of her mother's old nightgowns. She could still smell her mother's scent on those nightgowns. Maybe she was meant for something different in this life or maybe she wasn't meant for anything at all. It was in this mood that she took the safety pin from her hem and picked up one of the babies. She placed some tape over the places she would pierce and then she carefully pressed the pin into the skull of the baby and then into the baby's bottom. She put the baby's fontanel into her mouth and she blew everything the baby had inside it, every last bit of potential, into a bowl. She did it with all ten of them and took the bowl of goo back to the compost heap and said a prayer.

She was careful to wash the babies after that and she put them for a few seconds into the microwave in the teacher's lounge to kill any lingering bacteria and then she brought them back to the infirmary where they would spend the weekend being cured.

On Monday morning she came in early and the teacher let her go down to the cafetorium with some poster paints and glitter. The doctor had some of her mother's clear nail polish in the pocket of her white lab coat, an old shirt that had belonged to her mother. It took her about an hour to paint each one of the babies, each a glorious rich gem or Easter color with dots of glitter and glue. She covered them with nail polish to make them stronger. They were empty inside but they were so very beautiful now. She carried them back to the classroom and distributed the marvels to their parents. Don't cry, she told them. See how light they are? Their spirits have gone to heaven with the others. They're angels now, and nothing will hurt them, she lied. They're watching over you and loving you, she lied. What you're holding is just the beautiful reminder of where the life used to be. There's no more suffering for them, so please don't cry. See how they sparkle? Even if you crush them, they'll be beautiful.

The Plume

FROM THE OUTSIDE, THE GARDEN CITY CHURCH of Christ looks like any small rural church. The building is just large enough for a sanctuary, a small vestibule where the greeters stand, an office in the back, and a basement where the choir practices and Sunday school classes and church dinners are held. Four steps lead to the front door, the exterior paint is mildewed, the steeple seems tacked on. It's as though it's simply a part of the landscape that has formed temporarily, ghost-like, into the shape of church.

The same ephemeral nature is true of the other buildings and businesses along the stretch of road that forms the unincorporated town of Garden City. There are houses made with asbestos-laced asphalt siding, trailers on cement blocks, a pole barn used for motorcycle and small tractor repair, a small pig farm, an abandoned filling station, one or two truck gardens, a cemetery, and a drive-in restaurant that serves chili dogs and tenderloins and is open five months out of the year. Because the gas station and factory that created the plume have been excused from their responsibility, the government has fitted the drive-in with an elaborate water filtration system, as is true of the church and a few of the other inhabited buildings.

There are no hardware stores in Garden City, no clothing stores, no drug or grocery stores. Garden City, in other words, is just a strip of civilization along a strip of road, surrounded by dreaming fields of corn and beans.

When I was a child, and growing up on a farm outside of town, I thought I knew everything there was to know about it.

If you find yourself there now, you'll have to drive another twenty minutes or so to get to the larger town that houses the county courthouse and the factory that makes engine parts and still feeds and clothes and shelters everyone in the county to various degrees. The newer Japanese plants that make circuit boards are located even farther out in the country. They're rectangular windowless buildings with the company name in crimson lettering. These factories seem to appear overnight as though pushed up through the soil by an underground rectangle, like those sculptures made on pinscreens. You know the ones—where you can press the pins from underneath with your hand and suddenly there's a 3-D impression of your hand. Take your hand away, push the pins gently, and it's as though you were never there at all.

If you're an executive at the engine factory, you're originally from one of the coasts, and if you're an executive at one of the new Japanese plants, you're either from Japan or one of the coasts. No one informed you about the plume before you came, and when you found out, if you found out, you were assured you were safe from it. The plume is nothing, primary leakage from the gas station and perhaps some dumping from the factory, you were told if you asked. It's a thing that happens everywhere. We're on top of it, they said.

In any case, you may have driven through Garden City on your way to your new home on the man-made lakes and not paid much attention to it. Or you may have passed through on your way to the tourist town that sells fried chicken and apple butter in the autumn or on your way to the university two hours away or on your way to the country mechanic, his yard filled with rusted parts and his helpers sucking down beer and falling asleep from a combination of the beer and fumes.

Oh, who knows why you drove through, really. The 'why' is just something we fill our time with, sitting on our porches watching the cars go by. That's what you think of us, right? That's all we do, just watch you go by, centers of the universe. So maybe you have a mistress or know a prostitute who lives out in the dark spaces. Maybe your grandmother lives out in the country. Maybe you're looking for drugs. Maybe you're on the lam. Maybe you're nostalgic for something, perhaps the Milky Way, and you think you might find it if you drive far enough into the country. I only know you most likely didn't notice that the place had a name and that the church was named after the place. And it *is* a place. It is *deeply* placed in fact, as the church can attest. I was baptized in its pool. The church member who nursed my parents in their oldest age lives in one of the asphalt-sided houses. There are red geraniums in a pot on her front porch. The geraniums aren't real, and yes, she has one too many lawn ornaments.

However, I'll give you this: if you did notice the name of the place for some reason, you probably commented on the fact that no place in the world could look less like a city or a garden. On that we can now agree.

To go on: inside the church, the benches are made of pine, like caskets. The windows of the church are clear glass, the walls are grayish white, the floors are sloped and clad in worn blue carpet. Over fifty years ago someone painted a picture of a river and trees on the wall behind the baptismal pool. The river is chipped and faded, is poorly drawn but recognizable as river.

The white robes for baptisms hang just offstage, like sheets for a Halloween costume or Christmas pageant. Ghosts or Wise Men.

Why am I telling you this? Out of love, I suppose, for this little strip of human habitation. Out of anger. Out of the wish to confess.

Oh, where to begin? With the hundreds of saints who have, over the years, dipped their white robed bodies in the water of the Garden City Church of Christ baptismal pool, infusing sin into the pool like they were bags or balls of tea, emerging cleansed and holy?

The bitter dregs of our sins go down the drain every Sunday afternoon when the baptistery is drained and cleaned. It is refilled with water and chemicals every Friday and blessed early Sunday morning.

The water, by custom, bypasses the pipes when the pool is emptied and the holy water is pumped directly into the ground. The water, when it leaves the sacristy, rejoins the plume which is also, though little understood or talked about, its source. Was it our fault, the plume? Did we begin the separation of the body from the soul, the sin from the sinner? Isn't it human to want to be cleansed? To pitch the dirty water from scrubbing potatoes outside the kitchen door?

It's the plume I imagine now when driving by the church, when I sit in my car at the drive-in, eating chile dogs and root beer. I live farther out in the country now. Every summer my parents, the innocents, went to the drive-in for their anniversary. They brought me along. I acquired a taste. This was before we knew about the plume, though the plume was already there underneath us, phosphorescent, corrosive, on the move. Whale-shaped, the tip of its fin on top of the ground at the abandoned gas station then. This was when we still trusted all the wells.

The knowledge of the plume came slowly to us. I have to say that it appeared first in our dreams. We dreamed of feathers and tornadoes, of rushing water and wind. Then it moved from our dreams to our senses.

First, there was the odd taste of something like oil in the coney sauce. Had the proprietor changed his ingredients? No, he had not. He added more brown sugar and it seemed to solve the problem for a while. And then the slight odor of oil in our morning coffee, the film of oil we attributed to the coffee itself. And then there was the graying of the glasses of cool water that came from the sinks, the increase in precipitate. We were used to variations in taste during harvest time and planting season. But there was the odor of something acrid in the baptismal pool, something other than chlorine, cologne, aftershave, and old hymnals on Sunday mornings. And finally, later, the strong scent of oil and rust that came up from our wells and flowed through our taps.

For a while the preacher kept adding more chlorine in the baptismal font to mask the smell. He attributed the need to an increase in the numbers of those wishing to be baptized, to the power of his sermons which were, to be honest, never powerful.

When I was a child and the gas tanks first came down, when the station closed, there were pools of black sludge on the ground by the church. No real problem there we thought at first, nothing dangerous, a minor inconvenience. Oil on your work clothes, gasoline in your car, oil in the petroleum jelly you used occasionally on your skin. Familiar, the smell of oil, even pleasant.

But then, finally, we had to face it: the trucks that appeared at night, driving out from the factory. We knew what was going on. We all knew. Some of us had driven those trucks out to the dumping grounds, the expendable places. We just didn't know we would be added to the list so soon, that we ourselves had become expendable. And so we trusted when the company said it was all safe, that the gas station tanks were built for just this contingency. The owner of the station, now a vice president of the United States, kept making money from his failed business. His family was charged with clean-up, but the debt was too easily forgiven and the vice president moved away from the source, presented himself to the country as clean of every sin. Our sin-tinged holy water was so very pure by comparison.

The brain tumors came later. By the time they started blooming in our heads, muddling our responses, the oil company had been forgotten.

I am a reliable witness and what I'm telling you is the truth. The first job I ever had was on the burr bench at the engine factory. It was the job you began with and the one you wanted to leave as soon as you were given a promotion to the line. Your job on the bench was to take a chemical so strong it made you hallucinate, so corrosive it ate through your gloves, and to work that acid into the engine parts to remove the excess bits of metal. For many years this was done by hand, the rubbing away of the burrs on the rods and cylinders. We thought of them as the thorns on a rose, on the crown of thorns. We were doing God's work. You had to have an eye for it, a feel for the sharp places on the steel. You had to know how to apply the corrosive, how hard to apply the pressure so the engine part left your bench polished and smooth. What was left at the end of the day were the chemicals in a pool filled with dissolving metal burrs. It was not unlike the baptism pool, you're thinking. We thought. At night the liquid was siphoned into tanks and driven out into the dark country where it was poured into the ground around the county, perhaps behind the abandoned gas station next to the Church of Christ, perhaps next to my childhood home. Trucks come out at night and leave things behind a wooden fence. Who would complain? Who would we complain to? Where would our livelihood come from if we did? We would have done the same thing if we were the bosses. By morning it had seeped into the ground, except perhaps for the small puddle joining with the sludge or surrounded by a fence and oozing into the roots of my parents' sour cherry trees.

It took a long time until we understood that the acid ate its way into the earth and formed a plume filled with the dissolving metal thorns and toxins, that the plume was making its way toward all the water in the world, feeding off its innocence, waiting to rise from the ground like the tornado in our dreams. Honestly, none of us stands a chance against it.

What happened to Christ's crown of thorns? I used to wonder this. I wonder it still. It fascinated me, the rivulets of blood streaming down his face. Was the crown removed with Christ's body and placed into the tomb? Was it left by the cross? Might some barefooted Roman have stepped on one of the thorns and if so, was he healed or sickened? Was the crown purified by blood or was it poisoned? Was it broken up and sold, thorn by thorn, as relics? Did it perform miracles? Or did it decay, corroding everything it touched?

I think the latter. I think it became the first plume, and every plume after that one yearns to join it. It pulses beneath the ground in this garden planet. There's not much time now, so dip your body into any untainted water you can find, if you can find it still. It's coming to a boil beneath your feet. Purify yourself. Rid yourself of the complicity if you can.

Beheadings

LENNY LEFT THE BOX BY HIS LIVING ROOM WINDOW while he went to the casino, so it wouldn't arouse the kind of suspicion it would have had he hidden it. Sue said everyone on the street saw the delivery. Now everyone could see the box. Nothing important in this box! Oh no.

It was a tease. While you couldn't see inside the box from outside the house, my friend Sue had been there for something (she wouldn't say what) when the UPS truck made its delivery. She told me about the collection of heads inside the box and about Lenny's pretend cool when he saw them.

Didn't you ask about the heads? I asked.

No, she said. He shut the lid quickly, and I pretended that I hadn't seen them.

He's the kind of guy you'd discover had something like that lying about, I said. A box of heads.

They're not real, she said.

Sue was my oldest friend. That morning we were having coffee at the exurb west of the city where I live now and east of the town where I used to live. Lenny and Sue had been my neighbors.

The exurb's center used to be a small town as well, but it was surrounded by and part of the newest, laciest edge of the now century-long phenomenon of white flight. The exurb was known for its roundabouts and for its estates and for the bronze statues of ordinary "small-town" people doing ordinary "small-town" things, placed carefully along the sidewalks in the town center. There was a policeman with a whistle by the walking trail, a man in a suit sitting on a bench reading the newspaper outside a real estate company, a woman with a red umbrella open, rain or shine. There were frozen children playing jacks and reading books, a boy playing with a dog, a group of Dixieland musicians in front of the opera house. The exurb had an obscene tax base and superfluous funds. In the middle of the week like this, with everyone at work, there were more statues outside than living people, and they all seemed happy and engaged with life.

Every single time I saw one of the statues, for a second or two I thought that they were real. The artist's statement on a plaque near the coffee shop said that was his intention, to make the statues seem so real that they tricked you every time. I can't say I approve of trickery as an intention.

One of the statues was leaning against a storefront across the street. He was wearing a high school letter sweater, just watching people go by. His hair was painted blond. If I were still in high school, I would have been afraid to talk to him.

The coffee shop smelled like coffee and caramel. The coffee shop in our hometown diner smelled like bacon and the mugs were stained. The coffee here cost three times as much as any other coffee, and you had to pay for refills, but it was all mildly entertaining.

I assume the heads in the box at Lenny's house had at one time been attached to bodies, I said to Sue. I assume he didn't order them, but who could have sent them? Perhaps it's an initiation ritual into some weird cult or terrorist cell, and the heads will start appearing on fence posts as warnings.

Or maybe they're empty, the brains scooped out like the inside of a pumpkin, I said. You could put them in a window or on your porch with a candle inside and the eyes would glow and the light shine red through the nostrils and the ears, I said, until the heads begin to shrivel or the squirrels get them.

They're not real heads, Sue said. You got that, right? You heard me when I said that?

Their eyes were wide-open, she said, and their heads were bald. Babies' heads. Plastic.

You tell me why they're there, I said.

The coffee mug was warm in my hands. Sue was still wearing her knit hat. It wasn't that cold out. We were both wearing jeans, though we'd just realized they weren't the fashionable ones this year. We never knew things like that until we met at the coffee shop. You could watch all the TV and read all the magazines you wanted, but the important information, the things that kept you in your place without your knowing it, was communicated stealthily, by back channels on the money river. We were always surprised by how people in rich places dressed, by how they wore their hair. This year, the women wore yoga pants with expensive jackets. If they wore jeans, they were ripped to show their thighs. Last year the rips had shown the knees. Ours were dark-washed and tight around the calves, with no rips at all.

The bronze statues, on the other hand, were always wearing fifties clothes: the women in shirtwaist dresses, the men in shirts and ties or uniforms, the children in either their Sunday best or Huck Finn overalls and straw hats. It occurred to me that the artist, who was from the East Coast, might have thought we still dressed that way in the flyover. Only the Dixieland musicians were black.

Were there holes where the eyes should be? I asked Sue. In the heads? Or were the eyes painted? Were the heads stacked vertically? Would the eyelids close if you lay them horizontally?

Painted eyes, she said. Or maybe the lids were hinged. I'm not sure. I only got a glimpse.

Lenny scares me now, I said, wondering how she would respond. Hoping she would respond in a way that we could talk about it. About him.

There's a whole membraned bubble in my head, like a blister, dedicated to thoughts about Lenny as he used to be. Talking to someone honestly might help lance it, might help me figure out if the thoughts float in poison or in honey, if there's anything I could have done.

Perhaps it's a warning, I said. To Lenny. *Your head is next,* someone's telling him.

You shouldn't joke about beheadings, Sue said.

Sue had taken on an air of offended self-righteousness and a kind of pious, false sadness. It was one of those instantaneously fleeting things in the facial muscles. I think she thought she should be feeling more than she was about to reveal that she was feeling.

I'm offended, she said. You're taking this too lightly.

I take everything lightly, I said. You know that. I always have. Just give me a second to compose myself, I said.

You'll remember, Sue said, it was a boy from my church who was beheaded by the Islamic State. It was only five years ago.

That changed the tone of our conversation completely.

The boy's parents had to spend a year pretending they were Muslim while their son was in captivity. The parents' eyes were so serious and frightened when you saw them on the local news.

I forgot, I said.

How is it possible to forget things like that so soon? I wondered. Like how many people were killed by that shooter in Las Vegas? What happened in Charlottesville? What was the name of that grade school where all the children were shot? What about the movie theater with the shooter who looked like a clown? Where did that happen, and when? How horrible did things have to be to stick in the memory? I asked Sue. Or how close?

I didn't know the boy well, she reminded me, but I knew his parents well enough to take a casserole, and anyone from the church would be bothered by someone laughing at the idea of beheadings this close to the event, especially from an outsider.

But of course you wouldn't know that, she said, since you no longer go to church.

From this point on, I said, I will never ever laugh about doll heads arriving at a crack dealer's house.

I had always been one to laugh at inappropriate times, like now, when I felt uncomfortable. I molded my face. *Woman Listening Intently to Her Dearest Friend*, the artist would title us.

And I'm not an outsider, I said. You know I'm not.

I'm not always so sure, Sue said. She looked out the window. She had gotten so thin over the past year.

It was all so gruesome, she said, uncivilized.

I remember, I said.

I followed her eyes out the window. The policeman hadn't moved from his spot at the crosswalk, and he never would.

What was heartbreaking was watching the boy's mother with her head wrapped in a scarf, begging for her son's release, the father looking so completely American, all of it interspersed with the grainy threats from the other side of the world. Like the terrorists were going to be fooled by the play-acting, we said at the time.

Maybe they weren't playacting, Sue said. Maybe they really did convert and wanted to believe their son would be fine.

Though, let's say they were pretending. If they hadn't played the part, and it might have helped in any small way, how would they have felt later? It was about all they could do, other than feeling helpless.

Their boy was sweet and young, but the family didn't know anyone important in government or the media, and they weren't beautiful people, or young themselves, so their act was for the most part unseen by anyone but us. It's awful when no one with any power to do anything sees you, and you don't have the power to do anything on your own. You never get quite used to the knowledge that you're invisible until it's brought home to you like this. Because while your life is going on, it feels like you're at the center of the universe. Most of the world's population seems to live that way, I realized then, feeling unseen by anyone who might have the power to help them.

I looked down at my phone and tapped on the browser. There were other things going on in the world at the same time he was kidnapped, so it didn't make the news as often as it might, I said to Sue. That Malaysian airplane disappeared the same year. There was Ferguson. There was Ebola. Robin Williams died. There were so many journalists and aid workers beheaded that they weren't listed individually on roundups of the year's news. He was one of many. I told Sue what I was finding while I googled. She sat there patiently, sipping her coffee slowly and drinking the free water. I didn't want her to think I wasn't paying any attention to her.

I forgot about Robin Williams, she said.

I forgot about Ebola, I said.

The beheaded boy had been a devout Christian and then a devout Muslim, we agreed. Really, he was. He would have been a devout Jew. We believe that. He just wanted to be kind and loving and help the poor and contribute to world peace and mend the broken. He could have been Jesus. He could have been Muhammad or the Dalai Lama. He could have been Abraham Lincoln or St. Francis.

I didn't tell Sue that I was now looking at the terrorist's video.

The boy wore a red jumpsuit. The video showed him being pushed toward the killing field. His head was bare and pale, almost obscene next to the terrorists, who were dressed in black robes, their faces covered by cloth. They seemed substantial. He seemed washed-out. The killer's hand was on the back of the boy's neck, and he carried a knife rather than the sword or axe I'd expected. There were no swords anywhere. There were no axes.

The beheading was carried out by boys playing at being men. They played at guns and knives and bombs and in the middle of pretending they stopped pretending. And after the beheading, his parents stopped pretending too.

You can watch the beheading online still, Sue said.

Oh really? I asked.

Most channels blur the boy's face the moment the knife begins to sever the spinal cord, she said. They sawed off his head with a knife instead of using an axe or sword.

I was still googling in the free Wi-Fi-filled air. I exited the video before they got to the gory part. I was afraid of what I'd see. So I googled beheadings. The usual people floated up out of the collective memory. Anne Boleyn. Marie Antoinette. John the Baptist.

In a beheading done properly, I said, the blood to the brain stops in two or three seconds and the eyes blink shut. The person being beheaded doesn't register what's happened. Though some clergyman did a *can you hear me now?* experiment in the 1600s and thought the eyes responded for ten or fifteen seconds after being severed from the body.

If you use a knife instead of an axe, I said, it's because

you want the consciousness embodied in that head to feel and watch, for the eyes to remain wide open in horror.

Are you still googling? Sue asked.

Someone should have gotten that boy out of there, I said. Our adults.

Someone should have taken the guns and robes away from the boys doing the beheadings. Their adults.

Boys aren't fully men, I said, until something closes in their cerebral cortex or someplace in the brain, around age forty or so. At least I think it's forty. And I think it's the cerebral cortex.

Please don't google that, Sue said.

And Lenny isn't a crack dealer, she said. He doesn't deal. He's just a bit lost right now. You know that.

I could picture Lenny's day.

Early in the morning, the UPS truck delivered a box to his house. And maybe because it was the fifth day of the fifth month of his twenty-fifth year, and there were twenty-five heads in the box, he went immediately to the racetrack and bought five five-dollar tickets on the fifth horse in the fifth race, all of them to win. Or something like that. Signs and omens and coincidences and conspiracies give Lenny's life whatever meaning it still has.

When he lost the twenty-five dollars, which of course he did, he went down to the attached casino where the zombies live. He wouldn't stay up top to watch the remaining races because he doesn't love the horses particularly, just the romance or rather the idea of the romance of the track. These are third-string horses living in Indiana barns and running through Indiana gloom.

You watch the race from a seat in a glassed-in stand with TV screens showing races with good thoroughbreds in other parts of the country, any one of which you can bet on. It kind of takes away from the sad real horses running through the rain outside the window. You wonder why they even bother being out in the rain, both the humans and the animals.

Of course Lenny bought himself a drink in the casino and joined the people in their wheelchairs, many of them carrying oxygen tanks while chain smoking, everyone stuffing animal grease in their mouths, dropping coins into slots in a dull rhythm.

The card dealers are all on TV screens and the cards are on electronic screens. This, I told him often enough, is what hell will look and feel like.

When I used to go there with him, the casino always did its job of making us feel rotten about the human race, so we felt much better about ourselves when we left it. There were rows of nursing home vans in the parking lot, not all of them for old people. He would be in one of them soon enough.

At some point that night Lenny would come home and do something with the heads in his living room, and whatever it was he did, he would lie about it and Sue would believe him.

It takes distance to get away from someone like Lenny. You have to really want to.

Lenny has guns and chemicals hidden around his house. He keeps the guns to protect himself from the zombie apocalypse which, unlike the zombies in the casino, will consist of hordes of dark-skinned people coming from the city and from other countries to take his stuff when theirs runs out because, you know, plagues or nuclear detonations or the power grid coming unattached. The whole scenario is imminent, he believes, and it plays over and over in his mind because something has to replace the stories he used to tell himself and something needs to fill the hours he used to work at the piston ring factory.

He believes that there are mostly black people in the city, because that's what he sees on television and on his weird websites, and there are white people like him out in the country, and rich people are scattered in between. The rich people want to help him but they don't or can't, he's not sure which.

But at some point everyone will need to get away from the chaos and violence that will overtake the cities. He believes this. He is prepared for this. He has expired army rations and a bulletproof vest and antibiotics and water purifying kits and bug-out kits in his basement. He goes to survivalist conventions at the county fairgrounds. No matter how the helter-skelter starts, it always ends with the hordes of zombies coming to his town and Lenny's machine guns holding them back and maybe, eventually, a statue dedicated to his heroism in the perfect new world he will help create when it's all over. He really does have this heroic vision of himself.

I could picture Lenny as he peered inside the box then closed it. Nonchalantly. Nothing important in this box! Oh no. He would have looked out the window as though he was performing for some unseen audience. I didn't know what the empty heads contained. But I knew what he was probably saying to the multitudes: It's what you want, right? A box full of severed heads? Look inside. Let me tell you. There are plenty more where these came from.

He thought I'd lost my mind when I moved toward the city instead of away from it, but I recognize insanity when I see it.

While I like the city, sometimes, still, I miss my hometown. I miss Sue and our easy friendship, the feeling that we shared a history, however flawed. And I miss the sky, so clear that you can see the stars at night.

Sitting in the coffee shop drinking coffee we couldn't afford, I pictured the heads inside Lenny's house. And while I knew that they were or soon would be filled with drugs, part of me really wanted them to be a sign for real and not just something in Lenny's cracked mind. I wanted them to be spirit-filled, benevolent. I wanted the heads to rise up out of the box, sweet merciful angels trailing christening dresses, floating off quietly through the window and down the street and through the entire world like Chinese lanterns, blessing everyone who has given up on this world, believing in their hearts that nothing good will happen to them again.

Apples

AN OLD WOMAN WALKS BY A CAR AND SEES a young woman bending forward over the steering wheel. Something glints silver on the young woman's arm. A bracelet? *Mama!* a child says from the back seat of the car. The woman bent over the steering wheel appears to be asleep. The old woman taps on the window. The child starts to cry, but the woman in the front seat doesn't move. The car doors are locked.

The young woman bent forward over the steering wheel of her car, the toddler strapped into the car seat in the back. The woman's skin is cooling. Her back is straight. She bends at the waist, her legs swivel where they're attached to the shield of her hips. Her skin is cooling. Her skin is cool.

She is so thin you'd think she had several ribs removed. You can see the knob of her shoulders. The child in the infant seat is crying. The mother's phone is ringing and she doesn't answer it. Her skin is cooling. Her skin is cool.

A dog runs by the car on his way to somewhere. The dog is heading north. The child in the car seat stops crying when the dog runs by. *Mama!* the child says. *Doggie!* he says. Usually the child's call would bring the response from his mother. *Doggie!* he says. *Doggie* she's supposed to say. *Ooh!* he says. *Ooh!* she's supposed to say. But the child's mother is in the front seat bent over the steering wheel and her skin is slowly cooling. *Mama!* the child says again.

The old woman continues walking. She sees the sheriff. *There's another one,* the woman says to him. The sheriff nods. He walks to his car and reaches inside. He grabs his slim jim. He grabs his kit. His kit is in a red rubber bag. He walks down the street to the young woman's car where the child is crying in the back seat. He opens the car door and opens the kit. He places a syringe in one of the woman's nostrils and then the other, hoping to bring her back to life.

The old woman turns a corner in the direction the dog was running. She wishes she could run like that. She has dreams of running. But her joints are seizing up. She waddles from side to side as she walks. She tries to stop the waddling, but she can't. It's her body's protection for the knees and hips. The town is a good size for walking. The day she can no longer walk like this will be the day she has to move from her house.

She is familiar with the sounds in her house. She is familiar with the smells. She is familiar with the flowers that return from the frozen earth each year and with the birds that return from the south. Up ahead, she sees another car with a woman bent over the steering wheel. She is becoming familiar with this sight as well.

There are two of them in the next car. The woman is slumped over the wheel and the man is in the passenger seat. Their eyes are shut. Outside the car, the leaves are lemon colored. Red apple colored. The color of ripe russet plums. Is the old woman the only one alive who sees this now? She must continue walking. No one will carry her.

It occurs to the old woman that there are no senior citizen dolls for little girls to play with. Why is that? There are no old woman dolls with cunning little wheelchairs and clothes that smell like unwashed hair for little girls to play with, to dress and carry. Oh, there are wizened apple heads and witches to pull out for Halloween, but there's nothing to do but let them terrify. No one loves them. No one is prepared for what she is becoming.

How to make a dried-apple doll:
1. Peel the apple.
2. Take a knife and form a nose, eyebrows, mouth and eyes. Add little cuts and dents for wrinkles. Stop cutting once it looks like a face.
3. Soak the apple in a tablespoon of salt dissolved in a cup of lemon juice.
4. Dry the head in a one-hundred-degree oven with parchment paper underneath it to capture any juices. Keep it in the oven for an hour or two then remove it from the oven and let it dry for a day or two.

5. When it looks like an old woman, drive a skewer up through the stem axis and introduce a small dowel to support the weight of the head.
6. Make pipe cleaner limbs and cover the limbs with a dress you make from a rag. Add a broomstick or a hat or other accessories.
7. The apple will last for decades. It will not rot.
8. But the cheeks, she can attest, will fall further in upon themselves, revealing the bones underneath

The woman in the car with two passengers has long brown hair. Her legs are long and perfect for walking. She's wearing heels and jean shorts. She is very beautiful, the old woman thinks. Two men are knocking at her window. *Is she a'ight? A'ight?* The door is unlocked. One of the men opens it. *You a'ight? A'ight?* He shakes her shoulder and her eyes snap open. She thanks the men who woke her. Her eyes are completely blue, the pupils specks of dust. No one panics. No one raises a voice. They have fulfilled their duty, the passers-by. The man in the passenger seat cannot be roused. He may be dead. No one panics, though the woman moves quickly now that she's awake. Her legs are long. Her fingers long and tapered. Her arms bend at the elbow. Her legs bend only at the knees. Her hair is deeply rooted. She thanks the two men for waking her. *Is he a'ight?* they ask. She gets out of the car and pops the truck. No one screams. No one panics. *He should be*, she says. *I know what to do*, she says. She grabs her kit from the trunk and opens the passenger door.

The old woman watches the tableau. She wants to scream. She thinks that someone should be screaming. Someone should be calling an ambulance. It's so quiet. Is she the one who's dead? She watches as the beautiful young woman blows into the dead man's mouth. She pushes a cap off what looks like the syringe the old woman used to give her children liquid medicine when they were babies.

Where are they now, these children? The purple medicine would dribble from their mouths.

The young woman places the syringe in the man's left nostril and pushes the plunger. She grabs another syringe and does the same in his right nostril. She breathes into his mouth again. She massages his sternum. She reaches into her bag for another syringe and repeats the process. *Come back baby*, she whispers through her lipsticked mouth. Her perfect skin. Her heart-shaped face. *Is he dead?* the observers ask again. No one screams. No one cries. After awhile the man wakes and vomits. The young woman thanks the observers again for waking her. It's all very workmanlike. There is no celebration after raising her friend from the dead. She gets into the car and drives off.

The two men continue walking. The dog is somewhere running. The old woman looks back at the first car. The baby has stopped crying, its eyelids dropped down over its eyes. The sheriff is still working on the baby's mother.

The old woman walks toward the convenience store where she will purchase a single can of soup from the jittery clerk and head for home. Yesterday it was milk for her cereal. The day before a tin of mints. Every day, she has a purpose.

Above her head, the leaves are russet and plum colored. The leaves are the color of lemons, the color of apples. Outside of town, the corn shocks are white in the sun. Soon the white winds will return. Soon the gray will come. But then the green in the spring. And in the summer, the deeper green. And over it all, the blue. Her skin is cooling. Her skin is cool. Why do the young ones want to rush this thing? As it is, it comes too soon.

She
Drinks
Too Much
of It

SHE DRINKS TOO MUCH OF IT. She drinks it from around lunchtime until she falls in bed at night. I have never seen her without a glass or jar of the fluid. I live next door, and I keep a worried watch over her. I am a bit in love with her, and I can tell you that she lives the life of a nun with the exception of the hour between two and three a.m. when she claims she is both lucid and god-possessed. He comes every night, she claims, the god, though she has never seen him outside of her bedroom, and I have never seen him, not directly, not at all, though I have tried to. I am the town folklorist. I am her protector. She is afraid that he might not exist except that he exists so richly for her.

Perhaps, it could be argued, she could describe her visitor if she had not had so much to drink. She is aware of this. On the other hand, she is afraid that if she did not drink in such abundance he would not come or she would not see him if he did or or—the 'ors' are endless. She could row from here to the sun and back with these alternative explanations. She is happy, she says. She loves and she works most bountifully. So I must be happy *for* her. She is thirty-five years old and exquisitely beautiful, as was her mother before her, and her grandmother and great-grandmother, well into old age. I collect their images. They dressed in embroidered gauzey fabric. Their feet were perfectly formed. They too produced the wine. Even I don't know how far back the recipe goes, or where it came from, though I have my suspicions.

It has occurred to me, as folklorist, that her mother and grandmother may have experienced similar nightly visitations when they were producers of the local wine, that she herself may be the result of one of those unions.

If I am to take her at her word. And why not? I refuse to believe it is the same god, though that is the way it goes with myths and gods, where every sister is married to her brother and every father is also husband to the daughter. The Pantheon is a small town, of course, a bit inbred, like this one.

She always leaves a glass of the nectar by her bed and it is always gone in the morning, so that is proof to her of the visitations. To the skeptic, it is proof of her consumption. Though her job is to produce and not consume, consume she does.

You have perhaps driven past the town and seen the winery, which is also her home. It's a small white frame structure located behind the Pentecostal and the Lutheran churches, along the old interurban line.

The house is surrounded by blue and green bottle trees, the names inspired by local flies, but literally consisting of ordinary maples and lindens decorated with empty winedark blue and seagreen wine bottles tied by fishing line and hanging from tree limbs, close enough that the wind makes a bit of a wind chime sound without much breakage. And yes, she knows it is a visual pun, the connecting of fishing line and fly fishing and sea and winedark and bottles and wine and wind (which, spelled the same, can still rhyme with wine.)

From this you can already tell, or perhaps you knew, that the wine industry is not as it is in other parts of the world. There are no sun-soaked vineyards with globular fruit, no picturesque growers and pickers or stomping and splitting of skin to mix the sugary juice with naturally occurring fruit-skin-dwelling yeasts. There are no wooden vats or even industrial spiraled steel where the fermentation, the must and sweet meet and at times form mead. There are no oak barrels. There is no bottling machine and, except for purely decorative glass hanging on purely decorative trees, there are no glass bottles. She uses two-liter plastic bottles from the town recycling for her work. They are quite functional. This is the one variant from the matriarchal line, her own innovation. She sterilizes the bottles before bottling, and there is a satisfying thunking sound as the plastic bottle sucks in on itself during the last burst of fermentation, an exhalation of breath that causes the bottle to tighten then expand and pop, the sound like a lid during the canning process. The cap serves in this case as the cork.

Of course the part of each batch she drinks herself is fermented and stored in damask glass jelly jars. The wine is sometimes gold and sometimes the odd amber of animal eyes: dogs, domestic cats, eagles, pigeons, and fish. There is one varietal that is the gray you might get if you mixed the Midwestern/

Siberian winter sky and a Shakespearean actress's eyes with water from Lake Erie. It is a favorite with the town's depressives, of which there are many. It lifts their spirits.

The process of making is quite simple. The sugars are from local flowering weeds. There are other sources of sugar, some quite secret, though much is simply her own harvest of honey mixed with rainwater. The yeasts are all airborne. It is thought by some that the most fruitful yeasts originate on her skin. There are plates of mashed flowers and other sweets around her kitchen. When the mixture on a plate begins to bubble, she knows it's ready. The air is always thick with yeast in this town and every home has, at most times, something rising or fermenting either purposefully or otherwise. Fungi in general are plentiful here. Morels and truffles have been given to us in abundance but also the toadstool with its soft mole skin and powdery deckled gills, the beautiful but deadly spotted red mushrooms that are so fetishized in fairy tales and the spreading yellow slop that appears after heavy rains and creeps up the aluminum siding of the houses. More mushrooms spring up under trees, beneath mayapples, and they join tentacled hands underneath the soil. They are larger than all of us finally, and more powerful, and we have learned how to live with them.

But I digress. One unusual part of the process is the boys who line up at her house at dusk to get the two-liter bottles. There are a dozen or so of these boys. They tie the bottles to the back of their bicycles and they ride carefully over the bumpy abandoned railroad tracks and through the streets, colored ribbons streaming from their handlebars. This is the way meth is shaken in small towns, you might have heard. But this is not meth she is making. This is ambrosia made from sugars and yeast, from flowering weeds and berries and the spinning silver wheels of bicycles and the harnessed energy of boys and by our blessing as the wine travels the gridded streets. It's ready, our children say, and we give them the sparklers we keep in our china cabinets, and allow the children to line the streets holding the hissing stars in honor of the wine, wine which can only be made in this one place in the universe. It is the one true wine. It appeared only once before, at the wedding feast at Cana.

And no, I will not say her name, nor the location of the town, nor my name, nor any location where you can find the wine or the woman who drinks it. It is my secret. It is enough for you to know that it exists. So have faith and know that life is rich and pure and that while she sleeps I drink deeply and gratefully from the glass she has left for us.

Think what you will.

How much can the liver take? I am a folklorist. I insinuate stories. I import them. I find them, but I do not make them up. It might be said that I drink too much of them, of her. Am I a vampire? I ask myself that, but I cannot stop the drinking. It might be said they make me giddy, the woman and the stories and the wine. They're mine. She drinks too much of it and I love her and I am completely happy. She is the source, the muse, and she has no children. How selfish I have been, you think, how much I've used her. She drinks too much of it. I drink too much of her. We are not immortal. There will be no more of the wine when she's gone, after that final fermentation of the skin, the fluids, the eyes and breasts and the wheat-colored hair.

This Whirling Machine

EACH FALL, WE HANG A WINCH FROM A TREE in the side yard, tie a rope around a deer's delicate neck, and we lift her off the ground. It's my job, while she's still warm from the kill, to take the tip of a knife and make a cut from the pelvic floor to the sternum, careful not to puncture organs. Soon there's a coppery smell of warm blood in the air, mixing with the smell of dead leaves and woodsmoke.

My husband pulls the stomach and intestines through the slit I've made. He's careful with the edible organs: the liver and the kidneys and the heart. I find the bladder and enclose it in a plastic bag before cutting the membrane that attaches it to the spine. The bladder is like a balloon, lemon-colored and warm in my hands, the kidney doing its work right up to the moment of death.

I put the bladder along with the intestines in the waste pail at my feet. When my husband makes the cut around the anus and removes the rectum and lower intestines, these go in the waste pail as well. When I was a younger woman, I couldn't have watched this, let alone participate.

We each have our own steps in the process now, those things we're good at. He's the one who removes the hooves of the deer, cutting deeply around the elbow, twisting the joints, and snapping them off. His wrists are stronger. I make the finer cut around the neck and down toward the legs. Together, we roll the skin down from the neck, carefully like you'd remove a silk stocking, cutting through the slick membranes that attach it to the flesh, until with a hard final tug, we pull the skin off the body. That's when we see the white marbling and the meat, the musculature, everything beneath the soft surface. At that moment, the deer is transformed into venison.

A teenage girl sits beside a grown man in a car. His hair is the color of black mascara, but there are curls of red in his beard. The sun through the car window makes the red hairs glow like burning wires. She wants to touch the beard in the same way that as an even younger girl, she had wanted to touch a stove, knowing it would burn her.

The windows are rolled down. He's driven her out into the country. Outside the car there's the oozing rot of year-old leaves, and a sulfur spring-fed pool. She can see it over his shoulder. It's a kind of smear, the colors of the pool, the blackish green down deep inside the water, then olive green, then crushed-leaf green mixed with the color of antifreeze. And hovering for several inches in the air, a dusky gold, an optical illusion, water you could pass your dry hand through. It's what she looks at while his mouth is on her.

There was something so odd to her about looking down at the top of a grown man's head, she thought, sucking on you like a baby might. Isn't it strange? But you don't laugh, do you? When you can't see the man's eyes, the connection between the two of you is gone, if there ever was one. Sometimes you want it that way and sometimes you don't. You wait for him to come out of his trance, to see you. But when he came out of his trance, he didn't even pretend to look at her.

I can't remember the age at which the sucking begins to feel as though it's a pleasant tug at the nerves in the belly. Am I simply remembering what it felt like to nurse a child? I've experienced the tingling feel of the milk coming in, years after my children were grown and my breasts were dry, that pleasant pull between the breasts and uterus. But do you experience it before you have a child? I can't remember. Are we that connected still?

At the time all of this was happening to the girl, she wasn't even old enough to drive a car.

When he pushes her head down in his lap, it's a taste like metal, the smell sour. She didn't tell me this. I just know it. He chose her, she kept telling herself. I thought he loved me, she said to me.

Listen. Did you know how anxious she was to please then? How scared? How fragile? How much love she had to give? Did you know she spent the week before Valentine's Day that year cutting hearts out of red paper and lace? That sometimes when I woke her up for school I would look down at her where she held the satin edge of her blanket by her face, her thumb so near her mouth, making those clicking sounds in her throat like she had as a baby still at the breast.

He first kissed her in the school's darkroom. She was flattered. I would do anything he asked, she wrote in her diary, and she did. She would stay late, working on the yearbook. That's what she told her father and me. He loved to take chances, the man, to push her against the wall and lift her skirt like in the movies. Before him, she had worn only jeans and sweats. She dressed now for him. She became a caricature of a schoolgirl. *Hit me baby.*

This went on, I later learned, for several months. Life was hard for her in the remaining years of high school. She sulked, she cried, she withdrew into her room. The girlfriends of her innocence had moved on without her. Her new friends were fickle and harsh. Should I have known then what I know now? At some level, did I know? She came out of it, has a family of her own. Her own daughter is in grade school. Her father and I are retired, and we live in the dark place between the towns. She and her family come to our house once a week or so to eat a meal with us. We keep a freezer stocked with venison. We preserve the corn and strawberries, the tomatoes and apples, the peppers and cucumbers from our garden. At night the woods around our small farm are filled with rustling as the coyotes and fox and raccoons and possums begin their nighttime foraging. Sometimes I see their eyes flash, moon colored, in the dark, or I think I do. I sit outside the house and am overwhelmed at the intensity of it all, the predators and prey, the violent sounds of mating, the whirling machinery of this terrifying place, and my family, my responsibility, in the middle of it all. *The body of Christ, broken for you,* I whisper to myself.

The blood of Christ, I say, *the cup of salvation.*

Last October we cut a pig's throat then hung him from a tree limb, the blood flowing through the deep gash in its neck. It was that same red that gets on your hands when you open the plastic from a meat tray, or pull back the white butcher's paper, or you surprise yourself with menstrual blood, but thick with clots. You rinse it down the sink and wash your hands with strong soap. And there it was, gurgling from the pig's cut throat.

And when the blood had emptied from him, we lay him down upon a slab of wood. I took a brush and razor and began working on the skin. For hours, it seemed, I brushed and shaved the hairs. I was tender with its body, so tender as I smoothed the skin, as though it were a child having some nightmare, and I was there to comfort it. That bloated body, it lay there like it was sleeping.

And I'm not, really, making the connection you may think. Of course there's anger still, but also this deep sadness connected to everything there is. To the one who does the butchering, eating will always be a sacrament. The flesh in the dome of your mouth, your flesh, this fallen world.

The Warhol Girl

THE SOUND OF A LEAF BLOWER. Everywhere that high shrill scream. The homes small cottages with English gardens. No visible places of employment. A high school but no children playing. No gravestones in the graveyard. No jet trails in the sky. An iron bridge over a picturesque river, connecting one state to another. No one passing either way since he himself crossed over. He was early for the appointment and hoped to get his bearings. The wind!

She had said the house was second from the corner, a simple brown cape with a rectangular dormer over the front porch. He found it easily. The gardens had been cut back for the winter. Pine needles piled underneath the rhododendrons. Leaves falling en masse from a linden tree in the front yard, like they were being poured from a bucket. Could he walk from the car to the house? What had possessed him to make this appointment?

He could. He walked. Head down. The wind. Yesterday he had buzzed his hair like it was in Iraq. He had ironed his clothes. He looked unfamiliar to himself. He smelled of soap. There were times he thought it might be easier to navigate this world now if he had a cane.

The leaves! The reflections of leaves on the blue windows of his car seemed less frenetic than on the trees where the branches were frantically shaking off the dead. Which image was the real one? The reflected ones were only bobbing, bobbing. The disconnect made him feel seasick.

He tells himself he won't look back at the car but he looks back to make sure it is still there as he'd left it.

And there is a crash test dummy sitting, staring forward, in the driver's seat.

He turns fully around and stares at the dummy's staring. It only takes a second to realize it is the shadowed headrest. Still. In that beat he thinks he sees the head move toward him. He thinks he sees the dummy blink. The silvered reflection of the leaves in the bluegreen glass give it mirrored glasses. The back seat belt looks like the back of the dummy's suit. The seat itself looks like his chest. Perhaps it was the accumulation of fumes. Years of fumes. They've widened the perceptual beat, that weird hallucinatory space only the artist and the mad were destined, it seemed, to consciously account for. Which one was he? Both, he was afraid. Had always been that. Afraid.

He rang the front bell and waited for the woman inside to answer. The wind. He needed to be inside the house. He was familiar with the house from the photographs she'd sent him. When women sent him pictures of their houses, there was always a ghost image of the camera-taking woman somewhere in one of the photographs: in a mirror, most often, in the glass covering a photograph or a metal knickknack or even an appliance. It was difficult to take an interior photograph without, at some point, getting a reflection of yourself taking the photograph. And so the woman who opened the door was not completely unfamiliar to him. A blessing. She had been wearing a loose dress in the reflection. The camera had been covering her face in the image she'd sent, of course, but she was dressed in the simple way of a woman who has always been beautiful. He could tell a lot of things from the way her hands held the camera.

Are you the carpenter? she asked him. She put her right hand up to shade her eyes as though she were looking out the front door directly into the sun, but today there wasn't a sun. He couldn't see her face in the mix of gloom and hand.

He said that yes he was. He stood waiting. What else did she want him to tell her? I've brought the samples, he said when she didn't ask him in and just continued squinting out the door at him. To turn around in the daylight, to walk back to the car, to make it across the bridge and then home was impossible at this moment, but right now making it across the threshold seemed equally impossible.

He reminded her he was there so she could check the wood and stain since the table would be made particularly for her space. This was of course a lie. A copy of a copy, Amish made, it was already in his workshop, waiting for him to apply the stain. You asked me to come, he said.

She backed up into the front hallway and motioned him in. From the photographs she had sent him, he expected light and air. There were floor-to-ceiling cottage windows in the living room and dining room, but today the shutters were shut as though the woman were preparing for a hurricane or burial.

They were at least five hundred miles from the sea in any direction. 6,624 miles from Fallujah. A relatively safe place, this. The center of the country.

The walls were painted, as he knew, a glossy deep green with white trim. The dark paint did not, in photographs, appear dark as in dreary. But with the shutters closed and the lamps turned off, it was in fact dreary.

The woman closed the door behind him. I hope you don't mind the dark, she said, and she pressed her hands against her temples. I think I may be sick, she said, and she walked down a step into the living room.

The floors were slick with shine. For a second he was afraid to step down. It was water, endless and dark. It is a floor, he told himself. It will hold you. Take a step and walk. He walked. The danger was of course that at any step it might turn again to water.

The woman lay back on the couch. How trustful she was. He recognized the couch from the photographs. She picked up what looked like a wet cloth from the floor in front of the couch, where his coffee table would soon be, and she laid it across her eyes. He worried about the damp cloth on the hardwood. Despite everything, he still loved the grain of wood.

There was a round black circle in one corner where a plant had obviously been. That stain would bother him. He would sand it out or replace the boards. He would suggest this. He would suggest painting the room a more cheerful color.

The tasks would add up, if she would have him. He had just enough energy to make it through a series of odd jobs before he hit bottom again. Perhaps she would care. Perhaps she had a spare bedroom. She would feed him and make the bed with clean sheets.

It will just take a minute, she said. So sorry, she said. This happens rarely.

Migraine? he asked.

She lifted her hand and made a limp motion that seemed to indicate yes.

It's the wind, he said.

He'd never had a migraine, but he recognized the signs. And it seemed like migraine weather.

She made another motion with her hand, again an affirmative motion.

Her legs were long and so were her fingers.

There was a piano in the corner of the room. An old Steinway grand. The black wood shone and reflected greenly from the wall. It was like he'd come in from the dying tones of a Midwestern autumn to something verdant. There were magazines and books all around the room, notebooks and pencils. There was a long window seat that served as a bookcase. He counted each breath. He closed his eyes and looked for the red spot that helped him meditate. It was there.

Perhaps I should come back at another time, he said.

She made a motion that seemed like no, though he wasn't sure which question she was answering.

Her hair was thick and long. There were strands of it across the couch pillow, like an arm. There was something seaweed-like to her hair. Perhaps that too was the green. Was it gold or silver, the hair? It had been hard to tell in the silver reflection, and it was hard to tell now. He hadn't noticed at the door. Her skin was a bit green as well. The color of mint. From an illness? He had been wrong about the floor. It wouldn't hold him.

Breathe, he told himself. Silver and mercury glass urns and vases filled a bookcase on one wall. That's where he'd seen her image, multiplied in the photograph. They appeared to be old, not reproductions. He wondered if mercury glass had ever been made from mercury. When he was a child he liked nothing better than sick days when the thermometer would fall and break on the kitchen floor.

The balls of quicksilver would roll together and form amoebas of silver. Quicksilver. How was it stored when it wasn't in glass? In some type of bladder. Like eye drops. Wine. A miraculous substance, quicksilver, but poison.

Outside the windows, the leaf blowers continued their alarm. When you took the photo of the room, he said, you had the shutters open. The windows.

She nodded.

Do you have auras? he asked.

No answer.

With the migraines, he said. He didn't know what else to say. I have auras, he added. He was of course lying.

Her hand said yes. His hands were shaking.

I have the ones that look like a fortress, he said.

Where had he read this? Was this an odd thing to say? She didn't seem to take it as odd. She had no reason to trust him, but she seemed to trust him. He had sent her many photos of his work. His student work. She had called him a true artist.

She took a deep breath. He could see her chest rise. Tea, she said. In the kitchen, she said. Would you? she asked. The caffeine. She had mentioned it in her email. You'll come for tea.

He made his way across the watery floor.

The kitchen was painted a lighter tone, but still that minty green. There was a thermos on the countertop and two cups. He opened the top of the thermos. He breathed in the steam, felt it warm his face. He screwed the top back on. The shutters above the sink and in the breakfast nook were closed against the wind and light, and there was more of the mercury glass mixed with polished silver on a sideboard. It was every-where. On top of the refrigerator, on top of the stove, in the doorless cabinets. Enough to kill a person.

Above the sideboard was what looked like a Warhol print. He had noticed one like it in the living room. He was close enough to this one to see that it was signed. He walked care-fully around the table to the sideboard to examine it. The col-ors were bright, pink and red, sharp colors against the dull green of the woman's walls. 1968. The year his parents gradu-ated from high school. He was struck by the mouth and hair of the model, a silhouette. The aristocratic nose and chin of the woman in the living room. He wondered if she'd paid for the portrait or if he'd asked her to model for him. Then again, how old was the woman in the living room? Whose choice, the woman's or Warhol's? Was the model for this print a daughter or mother or sister or the woman herself?

A Warhol girl. What had he thought of Warhol, back when he thought about such things. Art school. Before Iraq. He'd envied Warhol, surely. The life he'd had. The freedom, the notoriety. The confidence. And hated him.

The door next to the sideboard was closed. Cautiously, he opened it. On the other side of the door was a white room. Too vivid. Spare. A south and west exposure, floor-to-ceiling windows, obviously a room built on and then closed off. A bed against one wall, bookcases against another, and outside the uncovered windows a gingko tree, still yellow with leaves. Two sugar maples, red. Black-and-white photos on the wall. The same face. Something pulled him into the room. He walked quietly. Every one was an image of the girl from the Warhol print, or someone who looked exactly like her, at different ages but always with a famous man. Some of them he recognized from school, or thought he did. Men of genius. A theologian, an architect, several poets, a novelist. There was a senator and a governor. There were men he didn't recognize, but they had a familiar look. Scientists or literary men. In every photograph the Warhol girl wore her hair in a simple bob. She was beautiful in every pose, in any light. In any era she would be beautiful. It was clear in the photos that she wasn't simply a decorative woman. She was in charge of the event. Intelligent. The men were looking at her but also listening. She was giving them ideas, and they were adjusting their own ideas in light of them, though they would never say so. No one would ever know this about her. She would be erased, of course. A woman who slept with men as they passed through. Muse. Siren. A wealthy woman with connections.

The largest photo was of the Warhol girl herself, arms uplifted, in a room filled with pillow-shaped silver balloons: Mylar or something similar, on the ground and floating near the ceiling and everywhere in between. It was an installation. There was a framed article beside the photo. *Silver Clouds*, by Andy Warhol. The Museum of Contemporary Religious Art. The balloons were kept moving by some unseen source of wind.

But it was the theologian's face that appeared most often in this gallery. He had read all the theologian's books when he was an art student. Art had been his ultimate concern then, and that ultimate concern, the theologian had led him to believe, was sacred. The theologian made him believe that he believed in God even though he said he didn't. It had comforted him all these years. Something to hold in Iraq, something solid. He'd joined the reserve for money while in school. And she, the Warhol girl, had talked to the man. And now she was talking to him perhaps. Here, in the pocket of nowhere.

He closed the door as quietly as he could and poured the strong tea into the two white cups. He walked back to the living room. He took a breath when he reached the glossy floor. It will hold you, he said to himself. In his imagination he could see the coffee table she would hire him to make and it was as real and solid to him as the woman or the silver vases, so he walked carefully through the space where it would be. He half expected the imagined table to bump against his leg. He put his cup on a coaster on a table next to a side chair. He couldn't see where she might set hers, so he held the scalding cup in his left hand and held the handle out toward her. Your tea, he said, and she held up the talking hand to reach the handle. He helped the two meet. The hand was papery. Was she blind? Thank you, she said.

I couldn't help but notice, he started to say, but she'd begun to drink the tea. He sat down on the piano bench and waited. He knew he couldn't make it easily from the house back to the car.

In the quiet, he pondered the girl in the print. A '60s hippie girl, she was at the center of the world for a time. She had left the Midwest. She hadn't been afraid. She had met the beautiful people, the brilliant glittering people. Her life had been filled with spangly silver things and white teeth in black lights and with drugs and anorexic longing. She was beautiful and fragile and fragrant and lovely and smart. He discerned that from the photos. And the collection of silver, like the clouds, the stars, spinning, reflecting light.

Was the Warhol girl the same girl as the one in the photographs and was she lying there on the couch in front of him? How old would that make her now? Did he hate or love her? It was too dark to tell.

He had wanted to be someplace like that once, to be that high with art and life, the way he had been in art school.

Yes, for a while he had been like that! The tea was doing some kind of mojo on him. He wondered, not for the first time, if his madness was nothing more than fear of madness. No, it had almost killed him.

After the military he had come back here for good, here in the center of the country. Less dangerous.

I was an artist once, he said to the woman, gesturing to the lithograph. I was, in fact, very good at what I did. For a time, he said. I was very good.

He put his hand over his mouth to stop himself from talking, but he kept on talking through his hand. Was he talking out loud so she could hear or just talking in his head?

For a while I painted houses, he said. To make money while I did my own work.

There is nothing more intimate, he thought, than the relationship between a painter and the woman whose house he is painting.

And then he started woodworking until he realized he could get furniture just as cheaply from other craftsmen and put all his energy into selling. I'm a sculptor, he added. Or was, he added, truthfully.

But you're still an artist, the woman said. Her voice was melodic, haunting, like a poet's.

Oh no, he said. At some point I realized I will never have my work in a museum. I would not be in the canon of artists. As the styles change, my tables will end up in landfills, no matter how much time I spend on them.

Why did he feel the need to disparage his own work to this woman? He had made the originals in the photos she sent him, even if he sold copies when he could get away with it. She wouldn't buy anything from him now. But he felt that, with her, he could go back to his true work. It seemed that he had fallen in love with her photograph. This was not good. It was never a good sign when he felt himself falling in love. He was in real danger now. He had never made a single true thing, however, unless he was in love.

But that arc upward that came with love would not stop with the thing made. It was an explosion that continued past the planets and the stars, to the edges of the universe until it fell back in upon itself, destroying the thing he'd made so carefully and leaving him shivering in the heat.

Was it Andy Warhol, he said, who convinced us that marketing is everything?

But that is not true, she said.

Perhaps I could have made more of my life, he said through his fingers.

She waved her hand. Quiet. He shushed himself. He would wait. What was her story?

Perhaps the Warhol girl had a baby before she left for the city. The baby was now in her thirties. She was as beautiful as her mother had been. Her mother was dead. The Warhol girl's daughter inherited the picture. She had it on the wall in her kitchen and this other in the living room. She collected silver and glass. How did she make her own money? She came from money. There were oil wells on her property. The woman on the couch, the one he now loves, is the Warhol girl's daughter, a trust fund girl. He had never known a trust fund girl.

Warhol sent her the silkscreens in memory of her beautiful hippie mother. She wanted to be an artist as well. Perhaps she was Warhol's soul mate. But art frightened her because of its connection with her mother.

I have fallen in love with a photograph, he thought. You mustn't be afraid of art, the Warhol girl whispered to him. You mustn't be.

So he had spoken aloud after all. He got up bravely, he thought, took the measurements of the room and the empty space on the floor. He had to leave. He left her with his business card. He ran. The memory of the Warhol girl got him through the next dark months.

Five months after the first visit, he returned to the woman's house with a table. She had been so patient. He had worked and re-worked it. It was an original. The copy of the copy would go to someone else. He had wrapped this special table in cloth and tape. He made it across the bridge again, drove into the pocket town.

It was spring and there had been a flood. There were sandbags along the river.

This time when she met him at the door her eyes were clear, and she didn't cover them with a cloth. Her hair was quite clearly silver, not mint green. The eyes were a soft gray-blue. Clouded. She both was and was not the Warhol model. He calculated quickly. She could have been the woman in the photographs but not the Warhol girl. She was probably the Warhol girl's mother. For five months she had been his muse.

He unwrapped the table carefully, like he was unwrapping chocolate, a holy relic. She had a trash bag ready for the covering. It felt like a winding sheet. All the leaves were long down, and they'd been whisked away to the leaf crematorium. They'd been replaced by crisp green. She had the top half of the living room shutters open to let in the pale light. There were thin lines on her face. She was in her seventies, perhaps even early eighties, several decades older than he originally thought.

She wore a blue duster. Old woman clothes. Still, she was quite beautiful in her old woman way. He would care for her if she would let him. Was it his only chance?

The shutters were open. She had already made the thermos of tea and had it waiting with the cups on a silver tray. There was something disjointed about the juxtaposition of thermos and silver and translucent white cups. The inside of a thermos tends to darken and chip like the mercury glass she was so fond of. That occurred to him.

He had put a sort of obsession with her into every turn of the lathe when he made the table legs. He sealed the burled wood with layer after layer of oil. It was the most beautiful piece of furniture he had ever made. Soon some factory in China would be turning out copies, but not one of them would ever be like this one.

She was suitably impressed. She lingered over the burls, the grain.

She had been gardening before his arrival. After admiring the table, she put on a large-brimmed hat. Straw. She took him out to the garden. The roses were uncovered. Soon they would bloom. What he thought had been her backyard was simply an antechamber. She took him through an arched wooden gate. On the other side of the gate there was a hosta garden and an arrangement of pear trees planted so the spaces between them were gothic arches. Through this garden there was another garden and beyond that the confluence of the Wabash and the

Ohio rivers. It was a sunstruck day. The river glistened like the blade of a knife.

I've never seen the Midwest more beautiful, she said, than during the flood. All the fields were mirrored with rain. The barns were in the middle of an ocean.

Did you know Warhol? he asked. It wasn't necessarily the question he'd been waiting to ask her, but it was the one he asked.

My daughter knew him better, she said. I introduced them.

Is that her portrait in the kitchen and the living room?

It is, she said. This garden is in her memory, she said. My little house as well.

So her daughter had been the Warhol girl.

The mercury glass and silver?

The silver clouds, she said.

It felt like joy to me, she said. Silver balloons. The Pentecost. But bruised, he said.

Yes, bruised. Still, she said. They were something a young girl would love.

In this, he saw the influence of the theologian.

What did her father think?

My husband, she said.

Of Warhol?

Of all of it.

I have a house separate from his. This is the house I live in. He lives in another house in another state. My daughter's ashes are scattered here.

Why did you stay?

Her ashes are scattered here.

Why did your husband leave?

Her ashes are scattered here.

How did she die? he asked.

She was a fragile girl.

Was she always fragile?

She was always fragile, but she was never afraid.

The mother of the Warhol girl walked through the garden and out the gate. He followed her. She pointed to the river.

Last night, she said, the Wabash was streaked with such bright silver it looked like you could mine it. The silver was the real thing and it went on, depths upon depths. If I had placed my hand in it, she said, I truly believe it would have come out glazed. And to the north, it looked as though someone had placed a painted scrim of gold and fresh green fields along the edge of the river; it was that surreal in its perfection.

That type of vision frightened him. It was too much for him. Like an explosion. It would knock him so hard he would never be able to stand up.

You don't think this place is beautiful, she said, but it is extremely beautiful. When you make something out of what you're given, you help justify man's ways to God.

The pear trees in her gated garden, trees usually so flame-like, had been trimmed to form a gothic arch between them, an explosion of arches that formed paper-thin waxed blue cathedral windows out of the night sky. The garden rested against her home as the daughter might have rested against her mother's arm.

They walk together through the town, the crazed woodworker and the Warhol girl's mother. He begins to see things he hadn't seen before. There are sculptures and small gardens, a stone labyrinth. This was the site, she explains, of two nineteenth-century utopias. And the art? he asked. I invited the artists here, she said. They felt that this place was a holy place.

Everything he sees is singing. Everything chimes, in pattern and variation of that pattern. The screens in the doors are gold and they glow and harmonize with the gates and an iron flock of birds chimes with the flocks of very real birds and they inscribe complicated figures of light in the air, like a figure skater on ice and all around him, the sudden glimpse of a brooding monk or child or woman or fallen angel—the mind's first draft—that makes him look again to see that no, it's no monk, no crying child or grieving mother, but a piece of carved stone. Too much. Too much.

This woman with the beautiful translucent skin, the extraordinary radiance, made this. She made this. Trust fund girl.

Did you sleep with him? By this he meant, and she understood he meant, the theologian.

He must know. He believed he knew already. She was the muse to famous men. She slept with them of course. She slept with all of them. Slut, he thought. Slut. The word gave him comfort. It made the place stop whirling, the gates and stones stop shouting. Slut, he thought again. She was now his muse. Perhaps he would make his own great art, his great ideas, if he could keep his balance. Slut. No. Tamp that down, something in him said. Please do not fly off, he said to himself. Do not ruin this, he said to himself. Be content with making copies and do not try ever again to become a little god.

He never embraced me, she said, never tried to embrace me. But he had that response to women that you felt that he understood you, he had that empathy. We were important friends to one another. It made his wife jealous of course, she said.

Once I was sitting with him at dinner, she went on, and we had just picked raspberries and I offered him a bowl of fresh raspberries and he said that his doctor told him he couldn't eat anything with seeds.

In the garden, she holds the imaginary bowl of raspberries in front of her and they seem real. She takes a deep breath to smell them.

I said to him that he should just inhale their essence and it would be like it will be in the next world where we have no need of eating but we experience the essence of everything good.

We talked, she said. He wrote. I wrote. We made this place together.

My daughter believed the stories about us of course. That's when she went to New York. She was angry with me.

But the memory of a life, she said, like the house of art, has many rooms. We fill them one by one and century by century. Most of them are locked shut most of the time, dust-covered. Make one true and honest thing, and it will live there even as it's forgotten. Now and then someone will open a door and flip on a light. That someone will discover some indescribable hidden-away beauty. That moment too will be forgotten.

They walked back through the garden and into the green living room. The mother of the Warhol girl picked up the tea service and started to put it on the table. This is where the service will go, she said. Let me take a photo first, he said. She sat down on the couch, behind the table. He took the photograph. He would take it home with him and work with it. He would add shadows and sources of light. He would carefully remove any images of human beings from the reflections. He would Photoshop the woman out of the image. He would sell thousands upon thousands of this particular table. It was gorgeous in that setting. The emerald green of the walls, the white wainscoting, the light.

The
Restaurant
With the
Glass Lamps

THEY WERE SUSPENDED OVER THE OHIO RIVER. It was nighttime, and she couldn't see the water. There was a blinking cell phone tower on the opposite shore, and he was driving toward it.

They were staying at an inn that was deep down in a Kentucky hollow, and she had lost the cell. There were pools of water at the bottom of every hollow. The pools were surrounded by plants with leaves as wide as paddles. Strange white air hovered near the bottom of the hollows, and all the phone signals in the world seemed to drown in them. For one entire night there wouldn't be a single thread connecting her to home.

She had to call her family. She couldn't call from the telephone at the inn because her home telephone would identify the number. She was supposed to be staying a hundred miles away. She had no idea there was anyplace left in the world where you couldn't pick up a signal. Somehow he had found that place.

This was, she knew, a problem only a few people in the history of the world would understand. In a year or two or maybe a matter of months, wireless signals would bathe the entire world with their invisible pulsing. Or something new would replace them. She was living in some kind of blip between technologies, and a Kentucky hollow might as well be in another universe.

He was driving a rental car, and the dashboard was complicated and hulking. She had never allowed him to drive her anywhere before. She was afraid of accidents she couldn't explain to anyone's satisfaction.

They crossed the river and drove uphill out of the boggy landscape. The cell phone clicked to life. But then it made another sound to show that it was low on power.

She pulled a coiled wire from her handbag. It's like you have to feed it, he said. It's part of my body, she said. And now the car is part of your body, he said as she plugged it in. And my hands, he said, are on the wheel.

She didn't want to make the call while they were driving through the country. It was bad enough that she couldn't keep the phone on all night. If she made this call, then there had only been seven hours on one side of the call and ten hours on the other when she wasn't connected to home. As soon as she made the call, she could relax. Until she made the call, she couldn't.

She needed to leave a message and possibly erase another one. He had called her on the way to the inn and may have left a message on the wrong voicemail, and she had to find it and get rid of it.

She had to remember passwords from three different voicemails and only five years ago she hadn't had to remember one. Each one represented a completely different world. She hoped that one or two of the worlds would disappear the night the century turned, though she was sure she couldn't possibly be that lucky. If all the computers in all the world shut down at the stroke of midnight, she would consider it good riddance. Wherever she was at that moment, she would stay there.

Her husband knew the password to two worlds and this man knew the password to the third. This is insane, she said. I know how you feel, he said, and she said I don't think you do.

The two worlds jostled against one another. One would attach itself to the other, one would burst, one would enclose the other—back and forth it went. The worlds opened out inside one another like computer windows with no beginning or end, only with that bubble-like membraney feel. She felt like she was slipping off the edge.

Just beyond the tower, the land flattened out into a row of strip malls and fast food restaurants. The restaurant back at the inn where they were staying had a wraparound porch and it overlooked the hollow. They should have been sitting there right now. But he'd left a message on her home voicemail and the inn wasn't in a cell and she had to make a connection to that other world, to make sure it still existed.

I had hoped it would be more romantic than this, he said. He had planned this weekend for months.

This night was as well planned as a crime, she said.

What exactly is a crime? he asked. Define your terms.

A crime's a crime, he added, and this isn't one.

Unfortunate choice of metaphor then, she said. She felt cranky. This was all too hard.

You think too much, he said.

No matter what else it is, she said, when you commit a crime you make some kind of parallel world where the crime lives, and from that point on you have to work like hell to keep them separate.

She had tried before to explain this to him. He didn't seem to feel the same way. She could feel generations of family looking down on her in judgment, exactly as though she believed in heaven or an afterlife, something she claimed she didn't believe in. And she had to say, she agreed with their opinions of her.

Just try your phone, he said.

She too was anxious to get the phone call over with, and he pulled off at the next exit. He parked at the edge of a convenience store parking lot, under a streetlight. The hood of his car turned an odd purplish black, like a bruise. He got out of the car so she could call without running the risk of him coughing in the background. He said he guessed he'd call home too, and he started across the lot to a pay phone. There were still pay phones then, at the turn of the century. She watched him walk. He was wearing a raincoat, and it wasn't raining. It was too big, was sweet and dear. He seemed oddly vulnerable. Sometimes she was mad at him because her life was too complicated. Then she saw how fragile and weirdly innocent they all were. They were like an extended family with this one secret hinge. There was something pulsing and cell-like about it, or heart-like.

She dialed her phone once, but there was too much static. She hung up then got out of the car and stood on asphalt. Even then, she had to face just the right direction to get a clear line. The tower blinked with that odd triangular light. A hundred years from now, she thought, when these phones are embedded in our heads and we can hear voices whenever we want to, this will seem like too much trouble. Right now, these towers always seemed to be either north or south of where you needed them to be.

When she got a clear line, no one was home, so she pressed star and listened to the messages. Sure enough, there was his voice saying he'd gotten a late start, that he'd meet her in an hour. He'd meant to leave it on her cell phone voicemail, but when she said she didn't get the message, he'd worried that he'd left it at her home accidentally, which it turned out he had.

It seemed no one had played it, though there was always the possibility that whoever listened to it had died or started weeping or was in a doctor's or lawyer's office now and didn't listen to the end. She deleted it, then called right back to make sure it had been deleted. Her knees got watery when she realized how close it had been. She hoped that deleted messages weren't ever accidentally resurrected. There were times when odd messages appeared on one of the voicemails, once when her work message appeared on the home machine as though that phone had called the other one. Once her cell phone had recorded an entire conversation she'd had with her husband when they were driving for pizza. It had something to do with automatic callbacks or pocket dialing or some subterranean computer hookups that she didn't understand. Now and then she felt this strange uncharacteristic paranoia, as though there was no place left in the world where she wasn't being watched. It could only get worse. Perhaps they would all get used to it sometime in the next century.

She called a third time to leave a message for her husband, to say she was going to bed early so he shouldn't call when he got home from work. Her husband was a lawyer. He would be picking the twins up from daycare, on his way home from work. The twins were five now, and they exhausted her.

She was fine, she said on the voicemail. She had meetings first thing in the morning, but he could call in the afternoon. Relax, she told herself. It's fine. You're safe.

The man stood by the pay phone talking and when he looked over at her he licked his own fingers and she knew what he was thinking. The only human bodies she'd known as intimately as his were the bodies of her two children when she'd carried them. She felt them move inside of her and then they were outside and the doctor held the cords until they stopped their throbbing, and he cut and tied each one and the babies floated out away from her.

She saw him hang up the phone and he walked back to the car. The night air was hazy, damp with the heat and condensation from the river. He said they should drive further into town to look for someplace they could eat. Her family could still reach her for another hour or so then, he said, if they needed to. How thoughtful he was. But what if she wanted to escape from this man? She couldn't escape, she realized. Even that would be difficult to explain. Who would she tell and who would come and pick her up and how would she explain how she got here without a car? Would she have to invent an abductor, one who drove across a river before dropping her off? For a second or two she wondered why she trusted him, how she had begun to trust him. And then she realized the same thing could be said of her.

The connecting road between the highway and the town was dark. He didn't touch her while he drove. She was grateful for that. He had just been on the phone with his wife, saying he loved her.

She sat down low in the passenger seat. It felt like they were in a plane, and falling. What an absolutely mundane and familiar story this was, how many times human beings had repeated it, each time feeling as though they were the only ones.

The lights of the town appeared like something on the ground coming up to meet their wheels. She knew they were directly across the river from the inn. She could smell the river mixed with the smell of the man. There were soybean fields right up to the edge of the town. The streets were empty, one main street with the businesses closed and a few globe lights hanging in the air. Did anyone live here? The beating heart of the country, and the pulse was faint.

He parked on a side street and they got out of the car and walked toward what seemed to be the center of town. Old houses, separated from the sidewalk by picket and wire fences in various stages of disrepair. They passed a bait shop, closed, then a locked bakery. There were white rings of dough rising on metal trays in front of a brick oven. Someone must be in there, someplace in the back. They passed a candy store that seemed to sell gyroscopes and chocolate. A couple of antique and secondhand shops.

For a moment the place struck her as charming. She thought this was a place where they could live together. Did she really believe that? She knew she didn't.

There was one restaurant, on the street corner. She thought it was the kind of place that served catfish and broasted chicken and roast beef and gravy on white bread. No one was going in or out of it. They hadn't seen a soul in this town, not one single human being. The name of the restaurant was printed in a watery neon green, like the name of a restaurant in a Hopper painting. *The Restaurant of Glass Lamps*, it read. It didn't seem real. The windows were large and you could see inside. The tables were spaced like tombstones. They were small and rectangular and each one had a white cloth and in the center of each one there was a lamp with a glass base and finial and a small white shade. The lights were lit.

The restaurant looked like a lamp store instead of a restaurant, but the light was soft and tinged with red.

She let herself hold his hand without thinking that someone might be watching them as they went inside. She felt herself relax for the first time in days, even though the town looked like the promised end-of-the-millennium apocalypse, the people raptured away but the lights still on.

There were no other customers. There was a bar in the back. The usual glitter of bottles and clean glasses. One silent waiter emerged from the kitchen.

The glass balls at the bottom of each lamp were about the size of softballs or snow globes. They were blown glass weights, filled with tiny pockets of air like the stream of bubbles from a scuba diver.

The light toward the kitchen was a deep red like blood in a glass vial.

Earlier that morning she'd started her period. There was blood on the bedsheets at the inn. There was dried blood underneath his fingernails. Her blood. That's what he'd been tasting. He liked it, he said. It was intimate. In other contexts she was a different sort of woman. It made her feel as though the real her was wedged between two others, that she'd become a small splinter of something larger.

The waiter seemed irritated. It was a few minutes until closing. All the locals would know when they closed, and there was no reason for anyone to be driving through here this late. He'd been ready to lock up. This town wasn't on the way to anywhere.

The waiter took them to a seat by the window. They sat on either side of the lamp. Up close she could see that the shade was made of creamy paper with flecks of something like eyelash. The glass balls were like fortune-telling globes. She put her hand around one and the glass felt good to her skin. The man's face was reddish-gold in the light, and the street outside the window was dark all the way to the river. They were up high in the middle of a cell and when they were through in here they would drive back down into the hollow where no one could see or hear them. The floors of the inn where they were staying were creaking and slanted and it looked like the kind of place that might burn down because of faulty wiring.

You know, the man said, I think this town used to be the state capital. It wasn't always this deserted.

The waiter locked the outside door. He would have to unlock it to let them out. Theirs would be the last meal he served this day. She wondered what she would request if this were her last meal and she knew it. She wondered if the waiter had a car and if she could say that she was being abducted against her will and needed a ride to a police station or, better yet, to Chicago. Of course once they got back to the inn she was absolutely free to go. She could get in her own car and he wouldn't stop her. She was free to go now, actually. Every time she thought something like this she realized she hadn't really made a choice yet, that there was still time to be a different person than the one she was becoming. And it wasn't all about the guilt. Here, in this world, she loved him. Or to be more accurate, inside the rented room, she loved him. There were times she could say that it felt, quite literally, like heaven. And what did she mean by that? It had more to do with solitude and intimacy, that feeling of eternity.

The waiter brought them fried biscuits rolled in sugar and water in glasses the color of garnets. In all the years they'd been together, she had hardly ever sat with him like this, in a public place, doing something as simple as eating food. In the restaurant or in the room, he always seemed comfortable. Perhaps he loved her? She wondered if her guilt was something he found attractive.

The waiter brought them salads with chunks of black pep-percorn, and they split an order of boiled shrimp. The shrimp was so plump and sweet she would feel the cool texture and tight rings on her tongue for days.

You know, she said, for nights I've been dreaming about God.

This is what I love about you, he said.

No one dreams about God, he says. There's nothing there to dream about. His glasses were made of silver wires and they looked red in the lamplight.

In the first dream, she said, I was lying on my back and I was glittery like these globes, she said.

In the dream, she said, my husband said you're in love with God, aren't you, and it was part of the dream that it came as a surprise to me. I mean, I didn't dream about God as something I could see, like a person or a painting. It was more like a feeling that my husband, in the dream, identified for me.

I wanted to tell him I was in love with you, meaning *you*, but also, oddly, *him*, she said.

But when he said that in the dream, about God, I realized that that was also true. In the dream, she said, I was aware I realized this.

In the dream I was lying on a stone, flat on my back, and I felt the glittering. It was like electricity.

In a way it hurt, she explained, and it was frightening but I told myself, in the dream, that I shouldn't be so afraid.

When I woke up, she said, I thought I might have come close to dying in my sleep.

She attributed that to some sleeping pills she'd taken, this near-death thing. Either way, she said, while the dream itself was pleasant, or at least felt meaningful, the feeling like she was dying wasn't. Though it wasn't unpleasant either, she said.

The morning after the dream, my mind felt shimmery, she told him, like a thin metallic plate.

She'd never had any dreams like this before. She didn't even go to church. She hadn't had her children baptized. She couldn't make it make the least bit of sense. Like this, she thought, like being in this place with you.

Some random neurons firing, he said. Some leftover day-time drek.

Some old message, she said. Waiting to scare the hell out of me.

Sometimes the world seemed stranger to her than she let on.

She wanted to ask him if they were still alive, if maybe they'd had an accident as they went over the river and all of this was just some waiting station, or if they were even in a dream right now. It could be as true as anything else, she thought. Clearly, she'd come unattached from something she had unknowingly and in a previous life been securely attached to.

In the dream, she said, I reached one fingertip out to God's fingertip, like in the Sistine Chapel, and even though I couldn't feel the touch, or see the finger, I could feel the tip of my finger turning cool, the way it does when you stand in front of someone's face and come close to touching it but haven't yet.

Or objects, she said. If you close your eyes and move your finger toward something, there's a moment of chill right before you touch it.

She closed her eyes and reached toward the lamp base. You have to have your eyes closed when you try it, she said.

You are so strange, he said.

And you love me, she said.

I do, he said. I do.

She knew this wasn't something he said easily because she had said it to him many times before he said it to her the first time. The thing was that she believed it when he said it to her and she believed it when she was with him and she said it to him but when she was away from him, she didn't know if she believed it at all.

She could say anything to him, and he seemed just fine with it. She didn't worry about him getting angry at something she said, or hurt, or thinking less of her. She wasn't sure if it meant that he loved her in that completely nonjudgmental way that meant he really loved her or if he was just at some level unaware of her.

Tell me something else, he said. He leaned toward her. They knew the names of one another's friends, of the books they were reading, the movies they had seen separately. They knew details about their childhoods, their childhood friends, favorite colors and foods. He had talked for hours once about the difference between South Carolina and Missouri barbecue. They talked about birds, about grain elevators, about light vs. dark shingles, about the histories of every country, about stones and methods of wine and beer making, about mythology, about geometry, about their children. Hours and hours about their children so that they each felt as though they knew each other's children and cared about the ups and down of all of it, the raising of them, as though they'd had them together.

And they talked about sex. That was his idea. Sometimes, on the phone, she told him how she came when she was alone. She made it complicated and drawn out because he asked her to. She could hear him breathing hard on the other end of the line, even after she changed the subject. She knew how he came, and where and when, and what his wife said and it was that, when they mentioned the husband and the wife, that the feeling of intimacy shifted to the feeling of betrayal. Don't tell me about that, she would say. She wanted to say. She never told him that any one point of skin on her body was connected by a straight line to any other point of skin, but she didn't tell him that at times not one of those points felt connected to her heart.

And did you think about me when you came? he always asked and she said that yes, she had, she always did.

She looked at the blood under his nails.

Whenever she came, she told him, his image was hovering somewhere right between her eyes, in the center of her forehead.

And what do you see when you come and I'm not there? she asked him.

Your face, he said, always, of course, your face.

Liar, she thought.

There were old photographs on the wall from the end of the last century. They were black and white but bathed, like everything, in red. The streets of the town were crowded then. There were giant flambeaus burning on street corners in some of the photographs.

A vein of natural gas, the waiter said when he brought them pie and she asked about the photographs. People used to keep their doors wide open in the middle of the winter to let out the heat.

The flames were blue, he said, and there was a constant stream of the gas, he said, like water.

All these glass companies moved here right before the vein disappeared, he said. They thought it was an infinite supply but the gas ran out in five years like it had never existed. We still make glass here, he explained, but it's out of habit and soon the factory will shut down like all the others.

There was a picture on the wall of white furnaces shaped like igloos. They were filled with some kind of hot soup that looked like it came directly from the sun.

There were pictures of men with long ladles like soup spoons, sticking the ladles into the kettle of sun and bringing out great glowing orange/neon globes of it. In one sequence of pictures, the men were running with the spoons, from the kettle to a metal table, and as they ran they were pitching these pure orange plasma balls an inch or two above the ladles and then catching them. The melted glass balls looked like they had burned holes into the picture.

There's a warehouse down the street filled with sheets of cold colored glass taller than all of us, the waiter said. It's something to see, he said. You should stay around and see it. It's like walking into a church, he said, rows and rows of color.

Sometimes a sheet will simply shatter for no reason, he said. Like a glacier, she said, and the waiter said, Yes, like a glacier. They just fall in upon themselves.

They give tours of the place, the waiter said. You should come back tomorrow in the daytime.

We will, the man said. We'll be here when they open.

She would be long gone by then, on her way back home. They couldn't possibly come here in the daylight but, knowing him, he would come by himself and be all amazed by it. He was still a boy. That was it. He was a boy and she was something else. A horrible person. You're one of the best people I know, he would say. Divided then, inauthentic, she would say.

When the glass collapses, the waiter said, they melt it down again into another color.

She could picture the giant flames of blue on every street corner. Like those brooms that blind men sell. The whooshing sound, the sound of horses sharing the streets with cars, giant furnaces melting sand and feldspar into glowing glass weights, the way each one flattens and clarifies so light shines through it.

You know, she said when the waiter left them, don't laugh, but I just want to land someplace on the other side of this stupid century and I don't want to be old when I get there. I'm going to bridge two damn millenniums with you, she said. Do you realize how very weird that is?

Everything we think and say is old before it begins, she said. Every curtain we put up in our houses, every cell and every breath, every single piece of glass or machinery that we covet, every car, every hair, every sweater, every sofa, every shoe, every story, every bit of stuff and every bit of goddamn guilt. It will always, all of it, everything we do or say now, be on one side of a century with everything else, whatever is coming toward us, on the other.

In the year 2000 I want to be born again, she said, or I want to be dead. Those feel like my only choices.

Let's find someplace to live together, he said. Let's buy this restaurant.

He laughed and leaned across the table to kiss her. Sure, she said. Why not. Let's do.

Tomorrow morning we'll tell them, he said, meaning her husband and his wife.

Tomorrow morning, she said. And this is where we'll live.

They were, of course, lying to each other. There wasn't a place in the world where she could live now and not be lying. And there never would be.

The cell phone lay on the table between them, hard -shelled and gray as an insect. No one had tried to call her. This was her last thread, her last connection before she shut it off for the night.

Maybe her husband had traced the phone by some kind of magic. Maybe he was just outside the door, the twins in the car. He would find them here together. He would break the door in, pick up the thick glass weights and send them flying. He would hurl the glass lamps through the air and smash the windows. They would streak across the sky like meteors. He would be like Moses in his anger with those flaming tablets. Everything would break and shatter, galaxies of glass shattering, waiting to be melted into something new, and she would simply stand and be in awe of it.

Instead, she knew, they would get in the car and drive across the river to the hollow. The cell would fade, the hum of other voices.

The next morning the man would drive away, and she would feel sick and empty. During the drive back home, what she would remember of the night is the boggy smell and the mist and the darkness.

A month later she'll be sitting with her family at a ball game. Dusk. The field lights will intensify as the sun dims. The lights will look like round glass eyes with metallic irises. The bleachers will be gray, they'll sag in places, whatever holds the grain together will have worn away on the surface. She'll feel the sinewy grain all petrified and smooth, but brittle.

She'll sit high in the bleachers, and now and then she'll have this vision of the whole thing collapsing underneath them. She'll look down the fifteen feet or so to the hard ground, nothing in between but air.

And the earth will spin, a new century in front of her. Everyone connected. And she will never in her life feel so alone.

Copies

Shortly before the technological revolution, I took a job at a publishing company in the middle of a small industrial town. Every day I sat at a round, wooden table with a rubber condom on my index finger, a box on my lap, and I collated books with a group of seven women as the table spun around between us.

We sat there, all eight of us, with this little flick of the hand the only real work we had to do. Now and then one of us would yell "Coming through!" if the ink was bleeding through the paper, and we'd throw a batch of pages in the trash without blinking. I was there for two years and I can safely say that I never read one word of one page from beginning to end.

And I never took one full breath of air. There was the usual stink of a print shop, the dust of paper and solvents and inks and flecks of metal from the Linotype machine and then the dust and smoke of all the other warehouses and light industry and cracking asphalt, unrelieved by trees or grass or even sky it seemed at times. The windows were high and painted over with thick green front-door paint, and the noise was a thunderous, at times metallic, hum.

All women, we faced each other eight hours a day, and had we wanted to, we couldn't look away.

We started each day with our complaints. About our sleep, our various children and relatives, our assorted ills. Someone was always sick or on the verge of it. Or we somehow looked that way, as the light on our faces was a flickering yellow-green fluorescent, like we were working underwater.

The men worked across the room from us, skinny boys for the most part who hovered over the cranky offset printers. There were two gray-faced old men who ran the hot Linotype machines and one haughty girl who made plates, all day long, a more vivid grass-green light flashing across her face. She was a person with skills, and she assumed we had none. That was OK with us. We didn't want skills. Because after about an hour of complaints or silence, the Zen of collating kicked in and we didn't notice her. There were just the eight of us women in the universe, and the spinning table like those pictures of spiral galaxies, between us.

Even now, when twenty years have passed and almost every face and every voice and scrap of language in this world rises up through a screen or wire like something coming to the surface from the bottom of a lake, or on the other side of some mirrored glass where you can't quite touch it, the impressions of two of those women have burned themselves into my memory. Like the hot inked metal pressed directly onto paper, an engraving of sorts, completely face-to-face.

Their names were Pam and Dee.

Try as I might, I can't bring back any of the other women. Faceless. Nameless. One with dark hair maybe, a little gray. One or two with young children. One, I remember, was nursing. I remember her space as wet and oozing. Too much flesh.

I didn't have children myself then and couldn't imagine it, the dark wet space appearing on the blouse over a nipple, unwilled, the quick rush to the bathroom to express the milk into a bottle to take home later to the child who was probably, at just that moment, somewhere, crying. That trip into childbirth was a journey I somehow couldn't see myself making. I was horrified by it.

Dee had straight, blonde hair, and she wore jeans and men's shirts, though what I remember primarily was her beautiful Slovakian face, and the way she stopped collating while she talked, which was often. We didn't mind. She was a spellbinder, and at the center of us. We were shadows by comparison. We would show a sliver of ourselves, or a quarter, or a half, but Dee was the full pearly button moon, full-out.

Every morning we waited for her to rise. She started each day with her head down, her hair in her face, keeping a cup of coffee in her left hand as she worked. None of the rest of us could have gotten away with it. Had another one or all of us sat there one morning drinking coffee as we worked, our bosses would have put a stop to it. So we didn't try. We just watched Dee as she sipped and the caffeine moved through her veins. We watched her come alive like some sort of Disney robot. Within the hour she cut through our morning sludge with her shining face. We'd wait for her to start us talking.

Somehow, that year, we became obsessed with sex, in its darkest forms. It had started, I remember, the day Dee told us how she'd become orgasmic after a girlhood of, she said, criminal ignorance, and how she thought that every girl should be taught to masturbate before she learned to walk. We had laughed so hard at that, a pent-up laughter, that the table had spun three or four times without one of us picking up another piece of paper. We remembered aunts and mothers and grandothers and cousins, wondering if we could tell, in retrospect, about their sex lives, thinking in our young arrogance that we were the first women in the entire history of the world to come, one by one, and without instruction, to a knowledge of our own bodies.

The other woman, Pam, looked pained when we talked. It took her weeks to get around to it, but she confessed there in the privacy of the circle that she had never once through years of dating and ten years of marriage and two pregnancies had an orgasm. She hated sex because of it, or rather, sex in reality; sex in movies or romance novels she loved. And she had kept the hope alive that there was something that someone out there could give her. These days she would have taken her problem to a doctor and found a pill or a program that might help her, but in those days we thought there was nothing to be done for her.

And Dee, I remember, took that as a challenge. She brought in books on female anatomy, she brought in phallic-shaped candles and vibrating balls and herbal teas. Clitoris, she said to Pam. Say the word out loud. Clitoris, clitoris. This was all so long ago! And Pam would look even more pained, but somehow hopeful, and Dee would tell her it was as easy as a sneeze, but even Anaïs Nin didn't have a clue, Dee said, you read her diaries. Once she had two husbands, one on each coast, and she didn't have a clue, which means that even Henry Miller didn't, at least for a while, have a clue or had kept her somehow ignorant. You know who Henry Miller was? she asked Pam and Pam admitted that she didn't. Anais Nin said he was the world's greatest lover and it was, Dee said, because he told her he was, and because he'd fucked so many women. Which is usually a sign, Dee said, not that you're any good but that you just don't at all even for one second get it. This all happened so long ago that we didn't have an idea women could say things like this. Were we innocent because we were young or because of where and when we lived? So much has changed in the world that I couldn't tell you.

And the table spun around and around, and Pam's laughter was tight, I remember, and too high. She was a nervous woman, skittish. Perhaps a little overweight, but with, as they say, a beautiful face and reddish hair. Inside the print shop she looked a little sickly like the rest of us, but outside in the sunlight you could see she was a creamy porcelain, that her breasts were large, not so overweight perhaps, just lush at a time when that wasn't popular. On breaks she always sat on the step nearest the back door, and there was chicken wire embedded in the glass, and I remember sitting there and following the twists of sunlit wire in the glass, the same twists like glowing sparklers in her hair.

Once I remember Dee reaching out to touch one of those twists of curling red. A strand of hair, Dee said, and I remember her saying this. So miraculous, she said, and at that moment she yanked one long strand from Pam's head and I remember this sharp cry from Pam's mouth, and the way she looked at Dee and the way Dee held the strand of hair up to the sunlight and twisted it, and the way it gave off different colors of orange and brown and red and even, as she twisted it, a purpley-blue.

We had two of these breaks a day and a lunch, like school-children. We were always sitting like that, outside, in the heat, in an alley by parked, half-sanded cars. We ate Milky Ways and sandwiches from paper bags. And always the smell, through the door, of ink and solvents and dust.

Sometimes Dee would spend the break running blocks to get an eggroll from a Chinese restaurant or a real fountain Coke from a diner, risking being late always, and always just making it, never content with what she brought from home. I envied Dee, I remember. I was hungry for whatever it was that made her so alive. I wanted to wake up in the morning and charge hell-bent through my days and never spend a minute doing a thing I didn't want to instead of spending my time, as I thought I was then, doing only those things I had to. When Dee ran, her hair blown back, she looked like a ten-year-old girl, like she was flying.

If there was a meteor shower at night, it was Dee who would have seen it. If there was a good band in town, Dee would go to the concert and tell us about it. I was always, I thought, asleep, or turned the other way, the one in a car who didn't see a deer or a fox streak through the woods.

Dee touched Pam's round arm as we walked back inside. It was warm, I suppose, from the sun. Pam's arm. Just watch your own hair across the pillow, Dee said, or better yet, close your eyes and put all the concentration in your eyes right here, behind the skull, from inside the middle of your forehead. And she touched her own forehead, right above her eyes and then reached over to touch Pam's skin.

You'll come then, Dee said, believe me. And she dipped her finger in wet ink as she passed by a printer and dabbed the blue on Pam's forehead, right where she'd one second before touched it. The third eye, she said, like in India, that red dot on women's foreheads. What are they for? Pam asked, and Dee told her they had something to do with marriage but that, in fact, she thought they marked the place you focused your sight when your eyes were shut and you were coming.

You know, in India, Dee said, all the nuns wear red.

You're crazy, Pam said then. And Dee said that she maybe was, *like a fox*, she said, and I heard her say to Pam that if worse came to worse she would have her boyfriend show her, or both of them would come to Pam's house sometime and show her. That is if worse came to worse. And Pam laughed and pulled a sweater from the hook by the door on her way back to the table.

In the middle of the summer we became obsessed with a local crime. The paper was filled with news of the trial of an obstetrician named Dr. Aziz. Every day I was the one who brought it up. Day after day we dissected it.

This doctor was Middle Eastern, "darkly handsome," the papers called him, and we laughed at the tabloid phrase appearing in the middle of the column of news. His darkly handsome hair, it was clear from the photograph, was actually gray.

Though that could be just the jail photograph, I said. It could be he was darkly handsome before his arrest. Or it could be, Dee said, that the reporter really wasn't looking at him.

That's impossible, I said, really. How could you not look at him? His eyes were large and intense and thickly lashed. I brought in his picture one morning and put it on the table, the edge of the newspaper tucked under a ream of one page of the book we were collating. Everyone took a turn letting the table spin without putting any papers in her box. You'd look at the picture, then put it back for the next person, like condiments on a lazy Susan. During the next break, Dee took Scotch tape and taped it to the table. For weeks he spun around in the middle of us.

Dr. Aziz was an old man to us, even in the black-and-white newsprint dots. Working in a print shop, we knew then about dots, how if you took a magnifying glass and looked at anything, it was never really as solid as it seemed.

At any rate, this old man mass of newsprint dots (we saw him, too, in the wavy dotted lights of the TV screen) was almost everything we'd ever feared, incarnate. He was accused, that summer, of everything unimaginable. Every day, there was something new.

At first he was charged with rape. One woman accused him and then another, reading about the first, came forward until there was a chorus. Lying on the table with the draped sheet where you couldn't see a thing beyond your mountainous knees, the women said, the doctor thrusting in one utensil after another. First his fingers feeling the outline of the internal planets: the fist-like uterus, the ovaries. Nothing different there. But then instead of a finger, simply—so you thought you were probably dreaming it because maybe, after all, you had dreamed it in the night, this darkly handsome man—it wasn't a finger, no, not the metal spoons. And you felt so groggy there on the table, was it that coffee he'd given you while you were waiting? That sip of juice? You couldn't see, you were so tired, the white sheet, and oh, his voice, not quite like any you had ever heard before. He recited poetry as he worked, he asked you about your children or the year you were in school, he understood your body better than you yourself had ever understood it. But was that his hand? Were those the spoons? Why were you falling asleep, so relaxed? You have to be imagining this. You couldn't see. You could be wrong. It was only later, when you read about the woman who hadn't taken the drink he offered her, who'd remained awake and conscious, who'd then become his lover and thought she was the only one. It was only then that you knew what had probably happened to you.

We talked about the histories of our own love lives. I'm not sure how it started, maybe one of the women comparing her present boyfriend to an old one, though not the way men might think women compare them.

We started with our first love and worked our way up to the present. We had these innocent stories by anyone's standards but we were all, it was clear, plagued with guilt, still, for high school midnight gropings, for a boy we let in through our bedroom window and who now made us shudder, most of our love lives a history, in fact, of guilt. Strange that it should feel this way, we thought, wondering why in fact it did.

There's a second strain, I said, a history of regret, and everyone agreed. And we mentioned all the boys we'd been in love with but never made love to because we were too young or because we had decided to wait until marriage or because we were glued fast to someone else at the time. "It's better to have more regrets," I said, and I said that I had never stopped loving the ones on the list of regrets, and that the ones on the list of guilt, though my list was short, I couldn't stand to think about. It does you no good, I said, to simply take a man and move him from the history of regret to the history of guilt.

At the end of your life, Pam said, I'll bet it won't seem that way.

I'll let you know, I said.

Though really, I said, my choices are always miserable. All of my ex-lovers are problematic. Alcoholism, drug addictions, failure. I couldn't imagine a life with any one of them. As though they'd all been falling strings, only one of them attached to a balloon and somehow I'd never chosen the right one. With any one of those men, I said, I would have fallen into misery. But at the time!

My God, I said. At the time.

And when we got quiet, I brought the subject back to Aziz. Every morning there was something new. His picture circled around with the textbook we were compiling—always something dull, filled with diagrams, a manual for some machine, a study guide for a textbook on snails. And Aziz like a hologram hovering in the center of it. No matter where you sat, or where the table was in its revolutions, his eyes were looking directly at you.

At least 100 women went to the police station to tell their stories.

He gave you his hand, they said, so gallant, when he helped you up or down from the examining table. He was so kind. He always looked you in the eye as no one else had done in all their lives. So they thought it wasn't real, what was happening to them. And each one who suspected it thought she was the only one and from that that he loved her or, at worst, that no one would believe her, that the evidence would never be accepted.

When we talked about Aziz and one of the printers would swagger by, all skilled and intent on an important errand, all Dee had to do was lean in conspiratorily toward us and whisper 'Aziz' and the boy we had just seen as classes above us would be felled with that one word, and we would see him unclothed, a male like all the others, so obsessed with sex that you had to feel almost sorry for him.

For a week or two, the news died down while they selected the jury, and it was difficult to bring the subject up because we'd talked through everything we knew. During that time, we noticed that somehow Dee was getting paler and Pam more animated. She has a lover, Dee whispered to me at break. She won't tell me, Dee said, she won't talk to me at all, but I know she has one. And one afternoon, in fact, when Pam had called in sick and I had to clock out for a doctor's appointment myself, I saw Pam walking out the front door of the downtown Holiday Inn. And I ran to catch up with her, but when I got within four feet or so, behind her, I saw that her hair was damp, like she'd just taken a shower, and she had that strong scent of motel soap, and I slowed down and let her go on without seeing me.

Soon the jury selection was over, and Aziz resumed his place among us. Dee became as obsessed with the news as I was. Day by day the stories grew. He was evil incarnate, pure and hateful. Did you read it? we'd say as we came in, shaking from the news and too much caffeine. God, did you read it?

The women patients he'd sweet-talked into thinking they were the only ones in his life and then trusting him when he said he wouldn't get them pregnant, after all, an obstetrician, he should know—performing their abortions in his office when they conceived. The fertility! No man could have this many unborn children. Every sperm he manufactured headed right for some poor woman's unsuspecting, sluggish egg.

And then one morning we read it. It was there on the breakfast table with our morning toast: the women who hadn't wanted to abort their babies and the stories. How he had invited them to his house for drugged wine, and when they had fallen asleep, had carried them up to a second-floor bedroom and sucked the baby or cut the baby out, the women waking hours later to a bed soaked with their own blood. And Aziz sitting by the bed, dutiful doctor, holding onto their pale hands and soothing each one, poor woman. The miscarriage had come on so suddenly, the clots of blood, no, it would be better if she didn't see the fetus. It was gone.

For years, apparently, this had gone on, woman after woman, until a woman died from it and the others read it in the paper and realized they weren't the only ones in his life, and that it had had nothing to do with love.

We talked about it as we collected pages and put them in the boxes on our lap. Some dry, disposable, textbook. Some unimportant thing. This was, as I've said, back before the xerox, the computer, before the internet, before cell phones, before clones.

And it occurred to me that it had been, all along, about copies, nothing else. All of it, this entire flaming universe was about copying itself before it died, that's all it was. And we were there in the middle of it, as blind to the machinery inside of us as we were deaf to the machinery of galaxies swirling in circles above us. Unaware at the time that there were new universes born each day in red and brown swirling dust so like the blood of pregnancy and amniotic fluid, the glowing wire of Pam's hair.

Who is this God whose image we're created in and condemned to follow? I said aloud. Who is it? And they looked at me like I was crazy. And I decided right then to have nothing in the world to do with any of it.

I was pregnant of course. Trying to decide that summer whether to carry the child to term. An orgasm with a child inside of it, believe me, is like an imploding star, congested and intense. The father was someone from the history of guilt. A small history, nothing as dramatic as Aziz. I never told the father about the pregnancy. In the fourth month, surrounded by the pounding of offset printers, I told Dee. It was Dee who drove me to the doctor's office, crying, though all she talked about was Pam.

And after that, every chance I could, I mentioned Dr. Aziz. In grocery stores and restaurants, to the checkout clerk at the drugstore, he became the center of my conversation. As close as we were, not a one of us could talk about what was really happening in our lives. We could only come at it slant, like this, perhaps because we didn't understand any of it ourselves.

Oh Dr. Aziz. If you had been some white or black old man doctor, someone familiar to us then, would the evil have faded into understanding, into compassion as well as hatred. Would we have spent all this time huddled around you or would we have faced the confusion of our own spinning lives.

Outside the town we lived in then there were fields and deep woods. In rooms all over the world there were men and women lying together. There was death and there was hunger and there was unimaginable crime. Someday we too would die. We faced each other every day and didn't talk of it. We pretended not to see as Dr. Aziz faded from the news, and Dee and Pam grew more and more alike and then finally changed places.

We never understood it quite, but eventually Dee married a firefighter, and from that point on it was all childbirth and children. She made an appointment at a fertility clinic in a neighboring town and soon there was a new content to her stories: surgeries, feathering estrogen and drugs, a new journey through all the dark and unpredictable inside. And around the time of Dee's marriage, Pam left her husband and headed for the West Coast.

The company bought new machinery and some of us stayed on and learned to run it. Some of us went on to other things. Eventually I married as well, and I had three children. And that was how it ended. The eight of us, women, around a common table.

The Dead

IT WAS AN INFORMAL WAKE, IN A RESTAURANT next to an art gallery. Binkley's was the name of the restaurant. It was also the name of the drugstore that had occupied the site in the fifties. The druggist's name had been Binkley, though no one at our table knew this, not in any profound sense of the word knowing. Nothing was left of the old place except the footprint of the building, and since no one had written a book about the druggist and he had left no record of his interior life, the restaurant's name seemed to be the pharmacist's only ver-ifiable resurrection. It's doubtful he could have imagined the gas fireplace, the minimalist black tables with their candles, the waiters in their white shirts, life going on without him.

There were pictures of the old drugstore in sepia on the walls, but they were purely decorative and not many people re-ally looked at them. They could have been photographs of some other place, purchased at an antique mall, for all we knew.

Whenever I came to this restaurant, I had a vague sense of having walked to Binkley's drugstore from my grandmother's house when I was a child and ordering a chocolate soda, but it may have been a dream of some sort. I couldn't look at the place now and say where the fountain had been, where the pharmaceuticals. And the restaurant seemed to be miles away from where my grandmother had lived.

It was the first day of the new year. One of our colleagues had died two days earlier. The eve of New Year's Eve, in fact. We were in shock, and grieving. The gathering was in his remembrance. We felt drawn together by this death. It wasn't called a wake in the emails, just an opportunity to lift a glass and mark a colleague's passing. Nothing else could have brought us together on this day, a day reserved for families.

Despite our sadness, it felt oddly festive in the restaurant, as such things do. We were teachers, and we hadn't seen each other since the semester ended. We'd had a chance to relax over the holidays. We'd been released from our obsessions, our student papers and our grievances. Everyone from the department had come out at the last minute for this. There had been thirteen of us and now there were only twelve.

There would not be a funeral for several weeks, we were told by the department chair. One of the dead man's daughters was in the last stage of pregnancy and couldn't travel.

The waiter brought our waters as we asked each other questions. Was he at home or the hospital and if the former, was his wife alone with him or was the hospice nurse there? How awful, we agreed, if the wife had been alone with him.

And apparently, according to our chairman, our colleague's death at the end of the year left the widow in a quandary over whether she still had health insurance, something she herself desperately needed.

Late capitalism is cruel to widows, one of the colleagues, a Marxist critic, said.

Life has always been cruel to widows, our medievalist said. Not in this way, the Marxist said. It'll be hours on the phone, a stack of death certificates FedExed to insurance companies, government agencies, credit cards with his name on them and not hers, all the grieving time spent in bureaucratic capitalist tangles.

Remember your Dickens, the dead man, a Victorianist, might have said, had he been there.

Who would teach Dickens now? I wondered. Or rather, who would love Dickens enough to teach him? Who would there be to pass on that passion to the students? No one could say. In the house of literature there was a light flickering out in the room of Dickens, a slight power outage for a day or two, since our colleague's passing. Any one of us could bring out the flashlights and candles, but no one could provide the illumination he had provided. It took years of reading to provide that illumination. It originated in the heart, and the mind followed.

Still, our modernist·said, so sad that it makes a difference whether it's the last day of the old year or the first of the new when he died.

Perhaps the widow should have hidden the body until tomorrow.

This from a Poe scholar, said in jest. He knew as soon as he said it that it was inappropriate. We veered quickly away from that thought or from asking where he was now, the body, if it had been donated or cremated or embalmed or was in some cold waiting station. We wondered how much our colleague had suffered at the end.

So here we all are, the department chair said. We made it through the end of the world once again.

It was 2013 and the world was to have ended in December, along with the year, but it hadn't. The approach of the Mayan calendar's end was the second or third end-of-the-world scenario most of us had lived through. Y2K, earthquakes and rumors of earthquakes, wars and rumors of wars. Apocalyptic fears seemed to cluster around the change in centuries and particularly millennia. Our students are fascinated with things blowing up and the world beginning again with them: against all odds, they would find a need for their bravery, a secret power they carried and had never been called upon to find. Each one would be an Adam and an Eve. Put the words 'utopia' and 'dystopia' or 'zombie apocalypse' in a course description, and the course would fill. One of our rhetoricians, in fact, specialized in zombie studies. The coming plague, terrorism, climate change. We all fear it.

We all agreed 2012 hadn't been a particularly good year. In part because the colleague whose informal wake we had gathered for had been dying for much of it and we had to go on all year as if this were not true. One or two of us had spent the year dropping by his house with food and watching his slow decline. The others had spent the year feeling guilty that we watched from afar, just asking for news. The occasional email, phone call, or card. What do you do in a situation like this? He was a serious, sincere man, at times a great man, living in a time of irony. What do you talk to a dying man about? What was good enough to say?

When all was well, department or college politics drew us together. Even when you talked about department politics among the well, it was a panacea, a quick rush of gossip followed by guilt. The sides were constantly shifting.

Gone were the times when you assumed everyone knew all of Milton, Shakespeare, or Virgil. You could mourn this or celebrate it. Most of us did both. You couldn't even be sure that each of us labored in one small unlit corner of that house of literature—an obscure poet, an untranslated Slovenian. Most of us still labored in that house, some of us one of the only ones in the room of John Clare or Iris Murdoch or Jean Rhys or Trollope: keeping the floor swept, the fixtures shining, waiting for some passionate young person to walk in and trigger the blazing lights. Come in! The shelves are full! And one room leads quite naturally to another!

But what did we have to talk about with each other? We had no passions in common, really, aside from the golden age of television—who was binge-watching which boxed set. *Deadwood*, *The Wire*, *House of Cards*. We could go on about television and film for hours. We had passions for teaching and reading, but our passions outside the classroom were wide-spread, too separate to provide a basis for conversation. One brewed craft beer and one made homemade mead from local wildflowers. One rescued mastiffs. One of us rode everywhere by bicycle and was constantly slipping on the ice or in rain puddles, breaking this or that. He was fresh off a concussion and was leaving in a few days for a six-hundred-mile ride through the Everglades.

But it all seemed so silly now compared to illness and death, things taking place on a different planet. Our dead colleague had loved Jane Austen as well as Dickens. He had taught Austen for the past few years because students lacked the patience for his beloved Dickens. He was seventy-two when he died, was wearing a leather vest and hat the last time I saw him leave the office. He was an early adopter of technology. He had a beautiful wife, beautiful successful daughters.

I had been his suite mate. For years he had hired a student to help him file his papers. Every afternoon the murmur of their voices talking about the student's future, about books, about art and music and the purpose of education; that perfect domestic murmur, familiar and comforting, came from the office and offered the type of calm I have only felt when I listened to the similar sound of my parents' voices, at night, when I was a child. That easy shift from subject to subject, born of true intimacy, though more father and daughter or son than husband and wife. He and his assistant would take breaks and walk to the student union for coffee. They would bring back plates of sweets for his afternoon classes, though he himself was diabetic and could not eat them.

After years of the young men and women graduating and a new one taking on the job, I had begun to wish that at some point in my life I'd had a surrogate father like that. It would have made me feel less lonely about the whole endeavor, shown a way. My parents read, and there were always books in the house, but we didn't talk about them. As a child I had read so ravenously but in such a solitary way.

This is what we have in common, I thought. I look around the table at my colleagues. How to express what it meant to work that closely to someone, yet not intimately, and to have that person, suddenly, gone. It was in the books, someplace. If called upon, I'm sure we all would have a poem, a line from a novel that might express it.

Should I, as his suite mate, put a sign on his office door? I asked. Will the administrative assistant, do this? Should I take down the sign with his office hours, the photos of his family in our shared outer office, his New Yorker clippings? Will his children want the clippings? The files and files of lecture notes? He was working on his autobiography when he died. How far along was he? Would anyone finish it? And how would I talk to the former students who, not having heard the news, would come by and knock, asking after him or those who, having heard, would come by his office door weeping, as to a memorial. It did not seem real to me yet. And what about all the books?

We had worked in such close proximity for over twenty years. It was an easy relationship, as we were both good-natured, though perhaps not a relationship at all in any real sense, not any more than the relationship between this restaurant and the drugstore. At some point he had withdrawn into his own work, the role of remote dispenser of wisdom, and that easy camaraderie with the brightest students. He was kind. I always felt I disappointed him when I opened my mouth to speak. Not his fault, but a lack I felt in my own education. I am a voracious reader, still, but an autodidact. I went to public school. I have read all of Chekhov and Willa Cather and Eudora Welty and a lot of contemporary poets and novelists but I have not read Thucydides, for instance. Never read Ovid. I'm always googling classical references. I have read as much in my life as I have had the hours for, but I read without a plan, moving from one shiny thing to another. Drop me a line and say I must read Thucydides, and I will do it, I'm sure, with passion, but then I will worry because I have yet to read *The Faerie Queen* or *Paradise Lost*, and I need to look once more at *Leaves of Grass* and for some reason feel the need, right now, to read about the history of agriculture.

My suite mate had a classical education, University of Chicago. He knew Greek and Latin. He knew French. He knew Middle and Old English.

And here is my confession. I did not go by to see my colleague in his illness. I called him on the phone. I exchanged emails. Illness removed the one ill to a battlefield, and I am afraid of battles. Reports from scouts at the front came back with horror stories of a hand too weak to lift a spoonful of soup, gallons of fluid removed from the abdomen. He had worked up until the day of his diagnosis, which came at the beginning of summer break. That was the last time I'd seen him, the day of the leather vest and hat. He planned on working on his book over the summer and had every intention of coming back in the fall to teach but was too weak by then. Just as I had every intention of seeing him until the end.

And he had handled that end, to all accounts, with his customary grace, even sending out a message to all of us explaining that he knew we would not know how to act and that he knew us to be fine people and however we approached his illness was exactly the way we were meant to approach it. He tried to relinquish us from guilt. I have never done anything with that much grace.

And so we went on with our teaching, our forming and reforming of alliances, our *next* day I will call him, the *next* I will stop by. I never had the sense of crisis. All of life is like this, I know from reading, but it didn't help. It was the sudden cutting off of those possibilities that seemed so difficult to take in.

So let me say now what I remember about him. When he was younger and his girls were still young and at home, he had given parties and his beautiful princess daughters had greeted his guests and given tours of the house and bookshelves. He had planted a holly bush by the front door when his daughter was born, and in kindergarten she was fond of standing by the bush and saying I'm Holly and I'm named after this tree. His oldest daughter took after her father and became an Austen scholar.

I remember most the stories of his southern Indiana childhood: the stories of abuse and beatings, religiosity and fraud, that went back generations. He worked his way through college as a fireman on a railroad. I remember him saying he was saved by reading, was given a scholarship to graduate school, and then after his marriage (which also saved him) and the birth of his first daughter, he experienced a conversion. The conversion was this: when he looked down at his first-born daughter's form he had begun this cathartic weeping that was, he said in later years, almost a mystical experience. He heard a voice, and it was his own voice saying *It all stops here, with you.* The horror of his family's story. And it did. He stopped it, changed the course of all of it.

If he was sometimes too aware of his intelligence, it was a minor flaw.

Earlier on, our modernist said, he had a tough time of it. Remember when he was department chair? Everyone was angry with him.

He wasn't born into sainthood then? a young Romanticist asked. There were the criticism wars early on, an older colleague said. We spent an entire year trying to agree on the Great Books list and finally gave it up.

And it was the beginning of the whole postmodern thing, he said. And creative writing as a discipline, I said.

I know, I said, that we were, the creative writers, at times insufferable. We demanded special offices, reduced teaching loads, better computers and carried, sometimes, an aura of revelation, as though we received all our words directly from the mountaintop. It wasn't an easy time to be department chair.

But at least we kept close reading alive, our poet said. Novels and poems *are* cultural studies. It's the writer's job to pull together the popular culture and people's lives and combs and brushes and *sidewalks*.

We'd had someone apply for a job recently whose dissertation was on sidewalks and strolling in early twentieth-century France. It was weirdly fascinating, I'd thought, but more as a detail about our times, the kind of detail you'd put in a short story.

Would you put that dissertation in your house of literature? someone had asked me after her job talk, knowing I was fond of that metaphor.

If the dissertation's any good, I said, it can go in the room with dissertations on urban studies, but not Baudelaire. If it is, in other words, a book to be read.

And what does *good* have to do with it? he might have said. Luckily, we'd already had that argument.

So. Here we all are, the department chair said again. Let's lift a glass.

Irish coffee, water, soda, a few wines, a few beers. Should we order some appetizers? It was late afternoon, midwinter. No difference in the quality or direction of the light from sunrise to sunset, as though the gray landscape was lit from within, on some kind of dimmer switch that made the day visible late in the morning and invisible again at night.

So yes, it was agreed that 2012 had not been a good year and that it had ended badly. A photographer somewhere had taken a photo of a wired garland shaped into 2013 from some small town's New Year's parade, and from the back it spelled Eros. We had all seen it on the internet. Every one of us had seen it! We were happy to be entering the year of Eros. What is it called? someone asked. That phobia, the fear of thirteen. Tri something, someone said. Three. Fear. Phobia. Triskaideka-phobia, a Postcolonialist said, pulling it out from a dark recess in the brain.

I'll bet there are people who came out from under their beds after the Mayan Calendar passed and dove back under when they realized they'd be living for one whole year in 2013, the poet said. Even skyscrapers skip that floor number.

But here we all are, the department chair said again, all of us here together. It seemed important to him to say this.

We talked about bad TV shows we had caught up on over break.

The oldest one of us, the Shakespearean, tuned out during this conversation. When it was his turn to toast our former colleague, all he could think of to say is that he and his colleague had always been in competition for everything. They were the same age. It was the first time any of us realized that the two hadn't talked in years, that perhaps there was even some resentment there.

There was a two-sided glass fireplace separating the restaurant from the bar. The fire was going. The restaurant was warm. It was a gray New Years, two feet or so of snow on the ground, beginning to turn sooty at the edges of the cleared streets.

So here we all are, the chair said again.

We talked about the musical tastes of the departed. Classical mostly, a lot of opera, but also some Diana Krall and Nanci Griffith. Sometimes his students would recommend music to him. He had been heard having a very serious intellectual conversation about Mumford and Sons, one where he asked questions and then placed them in context musically and culturally but was ultimately a bit dismissive.

You know when Amy Winesap died, I thought that was it, I said to my friend, the rhetorician. There would never be another somewhat contemporary/cool/hip heroin-addicted, bluesey, smokey-voiced person I could listen to over and over again on my playlist. It would be all really old and then really dead singers, like it was for my father. Frank Sinatra, Miles Davis, Glenn Miller for him. Mick Jagger and Bruce Springsteen and the Indigo Girls until they keel over for me. But no more new ones. No more romances for me, I said. Just passion remembered, nothing fresh.

Then along came Adele, I said, and she sounds just like Winesap to me. I mean, I've been married for years and I find myself screaming out "Someone Like You" when I'm on the treadmill.

Is it Winesap? I asked. It wasn't Winesap was it?

Winehouse, my friend said.

Yes, that's it. I knew that! How soon we forget, right? Winehouse. But there's Adele, and she's her own person only she sounds like Winehouse. Like Winehouse sounded like someone before her and on back and on back.

Who knows what fresh hell this year will bring? the Marxist said.

Dorothy Parker! I said. That's how she answered her telephone.

How do we know these things?

I was babbling. No wonder the dead man hadn't had conversations with me. There was some hope for the young women in his office. They were malleable, smarter than I had ever been.

I looked around the place.

When I was a kid I used to come here, I said to my friend, the rhetorician. Those pictures on the wall over there, I said, the ones that look so old-timey. I swear I was here when it all looked old-timey and it didn't feel that way, you know? It felt like a *now*, only I was a kid and this was a drugstore, not a restaurant.

I think there was a soda fountain over there, I said, and I pointed to a row of tables underneath a window. I would walk down here from my grandmother's house and order a chocolate soda, I said.

There had to have been some mistake in my hiring, I said. No one who was born here works here without moving far away first.

I know there was a mistake in mine, she said. They never hire anyone from Texas.

And I remembered right then the taste of the sodas, remembered most coming in here with my cousins and buying lined notepads in the summers. On the front there would be pictures of movie stars. Those summers I spent with my cousins writing secret thoughts in the notebooks and talking in secret languages and sucking nectar directly out of phlox blossoms. How long had it been a drugstore? A couple of decades?

It was rude, I know, but I looked it up on my phone while the others talked.

The phone took me to the history of pharmacy in our city. It was all there on my phone. It was in my hand, all the information. There wasn't a book, but there were primary sources. So easily accessible! What an amazing year 2013 was proving to be.

Charles Binkley opened his first drugstore in 1910, I read.

I wondered where he got his training, if it had been at the college where we all taught. We had the only pharmacy school in the region now. I wondered if there was a connection.

In that same decade, I discovered, the city's first school of pharmacy opened then closed down briefly then opened again. Mr. Binkley opened the second incarnation of his store in 1915 and moved to the location that was now a restaurant in the thirties. The Indianapolis School of Pharmacy and the school of pharmacy at our college merged in 1945, the year a man named Lill (whose recent obituary came up first in the Google search for The Indianapolis School of Pharmacy) would get his diploma and begin working at Binkley's drugstore. At the time of Lill's recent death he was the oldest pharmacist in Indiana. He died within days of our colleague. Two families mourning, the story of their lives brought together here in this one place in this one simple search.

All of this information was available online, but randomly, to be brought together in something like this. A story.

Everything in the world means something. Everything in the universe is connected. That's the real labor in the house of literature, I thought.

The appetizers were delivered by a young man with curly hair. Calamari, hummus. I put my phone away.

The older ones talked about colleagues who had left. Remember when so-and-so was chair? She was awful to the women under her. And that other chair, the one who became a provost at some college? We had a drink when he was gone. The conversation went in this sort of direction, into gossip and jokes.

The untenured colleagues listened to this, folk tales of people from some unreal time. Names they had never heard before. They could not possibly have existed and the stories were not interesting enough, not really, to record or to outlast the memories of the tellers. These people had been here and then they were gone.

Still, we all felt close, oddly closer than we had ever felt, like we were huddled together in a cave, a big wind swirling around us from all sides. One by one we would turn and walk into that wind. But not now. Not now.

And what I want to say is that it felt good to be there together in that place in the dying light, but we couldn't stay too long. It felt in those moments like we were in the same story at the same time. We held onto it for a moment or two like a breath, a prayer. We couldn't hold onto it longer than that. Only art could do that.

The youngest of us had children to get to. This has never happened before, of course, in the history of humanity, the oldest of us thought. Children to get to. Let's get another drink! The oldest of us had four children, grown, and not one of his colleagues ever asked about them, though he listened to their endless stories as someone had listened to his.

But why is it the bitterness that lasts sometimes? he wondered. Toward whom is it directed? There were times he hated the man who had just died, that aura of greatness, his need for an assistant when his own papers piled willy-nilly on the floor, the tops of every surface. The stories of greatness that would continue whenever his name was mentioned. And how long would that be? Would he too become a caricature? Would he be remembered as the kindly punster, the one who loved Shakespeare and a good joke? Would they all go from human being to caricature to forgotten?

We were all thinking the same things from our own points of view. I could see the thoughts on the Shakespearean's face. Behind his whimsical smile.

And how do people know when it's time to leave a gathering? How do you end a story properly?

The waiter brought the check for our drinks and appetiz-ers. The chair brought out his credit card.

While I was sitting at the table with the candles, the re-mains of hummus and crabcakes, craft beers and gourmet piz-zas, I thought about the pharmacy. Underneath the now or within it or existing in some ghost-like parallel past there had been another place: jars of medicines that looked medicinal because of their packaging or preparation; medicines that were in fact only tree bark, ash, lilac, poplar, ginseng, rhubarb, ephe-dra from China, fatty oils pressed by seeds, animal glands and dried blood, alcohol and distilled water; essential elements like oxygen, chlorine; prussic acid, tartaric acid, tungsten, glycer-in, nitroglycerin, camphor, morphine and alkaloids. Ordinary things, taken for granted. Culture and history behind it. The Shakers dispensing over two-hundred varieties of herbs while waiting for their own endtimes, explorers dispensed to jungles where they return with tens of thousands of herbs, chemists testing compounds on their own bodies, a system for coloring poisons, systems for inhaling oxygen, the glass ampoules for sterilization, and eventually the biological preparations, the toxins and compounds and antibiotics—taken for granted but somehow magical. All of these things had existed and they ex-isted still to slow it down, the ending of each story, to relieve the pain of passing.

Chemotherapy gave our friend the extra months that al-lowed him to make it to the end of the year, a year that had opened with such hope.

The word apocalypse, I had read in a student paper, is con-nected etymologically to the word "uncovering." We look at the world for signs that it all is ending. We change our sense of what a story means as we go along, testing hypotheses, and only in the ending does that meaning reveal itself, the possible meanings collapsing into one. Until then we make and revise guesses about the encoded meaning. Those guesses won't be satisfied until an ending reveals that meaning and retrospectively illuminates those experiences, "frankly transfigur[ing] the events in which they were immanent." Who am I quoting? A student? The rhetorician? At times it all merged together. At times all the books and all the stories and all the words and voices were part of one whole. There was no house with separate rooms. There was a swirling world of words and images.

And so. Here we all were together minus one, the department chair said as we began to gather our coats. Soon we were standing in a broken circle by the table. The Shakespearean and I, the oldest now, stood slightly outside the circle, like crooked teeth, like ghosts. We were on opposites sides of the table, would leave by two different doors. The Shakespearean tried to catch someone's eye, someone to say goodbye to. No one saw the gesture but me, and I couldn't hear him over the sound of talking. Goodbye goodbye! I waved at the Shakespearean. Same time next year, in different circumstances, the department chair said.

And we turned from the fire, left the restaurant one by one. Outside, in the twilight, the cold was bitter. And the snow fell on all of us, of course. On all of us, the living and the dead.

Parting

HELLO, WE SAY TO OUR SON WHEN HE WALKS IN THE HOUSE. His eyes look wary. We've met him at the door. Here, my husband says, please take my arm. He snaps it from his shoulder and hands it to his son.

I couldn't, our son says.

I don't need it, my husband says. Come in, he says, gesturing to the living room with his remaining arm.

You shouldn't have, our son says as he walks with the arm in his arms. I love it, he says.

He sits down on his father's favorite leather chair and puts his father's arm on the floor. The fingers try to crawl toward the arm of the chair, where they're used to resting, but it's too high for them. They twitch a bit, stretch, and wait to be called upon, though they're a bit put out, as is the elbow. I overhear their conversation. For over seventy years they've been attached to that other body. They know how to work with that other shoulder, it seems, throwing balls and unscrewing jars and until a few years back resting on an office desk, pressing keys on a keyboard. The fingers are worried.

I wonder whether our son will sleep with the arm, like a security blanket or stuffed toy, or whether he will put it to work around the house—put a glove on the hand and let it clean out the gutters, pull weeds—that is if the arm can figure out how to navigate on its own. I assume it will, as that arm has always been a hard worker, is skilled and obviously very bright, even without guidance from the brain. The fingers have played the piano, and they know their way around the valves of a trumpet, and a woman's body, as the murmuring of the fingers reminds me.

I thought you could use it in the shop, my husband says, referring to the arm which our son seems to be ignoring like he does most of our gifts to him, though not usually ones that are this generous.

We have been, I'll admit, usually a year or two off in our gift-giving: buying him a video game when he's outgrown them, cargo shorts when he's stopped wearing them. In our minds, he's always younger than he sees himself and in his mind he's always older. One or the other of us is delusional. Oh please stop, we used to think when we saw him grow several inches over the summer. We'd take out the video of him at three, sitting on Santa's knee and so innocently asking a benevolent universe for the things his parents would give him, and we'd watch it together. That's our boy. They were so cute, his secret wishes and thoughts, whispered to the red-clad deity so we could overhear.

The day our son was born, our hearts were ripped out of our bodies and placed in his like you would chip a dog. And he carried them so unthinkingly, risking our lives each time he risked his own. He's a bit of a reckless driver, and he breaks a bone every time he tries something ice-related (skiing, skating, sledding) and he has the unfortunate habit of giving his own heart to women who shatter it. Luckily he always has the two we gave him to rely on until he grows another one of his own.

He's in the middle of one of those heart regrowth periods now, we're afraid. The place where his heart should be is a bit hollow, and something in the way he holds his eyebrows has told us he's worried about something. He doesn't want to worry us with the thing that's worrying him, as he knows his worrying is contagious. But we can't stand for him to suffer and so we worry anyway. Of course we knew when we conceived him that everyone suffers and everyone dies, but we believed that he and his sister somehow would be exempt from all of that. Couldn't they at least be exempt from the knowledge of it? From what I can tell, some people seem to be. Exempt from the knowledge.

And how could you look at the little girl our daughter was, wearing sweet little outfits and going with her mother (me) to get her tiny nails painted for her birthday and imagine that the universe would allow anything bad like sickness or death to happen to her?

By the time she was born, our hearts had grown back enough that we could implant new ones in her body at her birth.

We've since grown our third hearts and we've had no more children, but they (our old hearts) are interconnected telepathically or by some sort of quantum-level weirdness to the hearts in our children. It seems to be impossible, for instance, for our third hearts to feel joy when hearts one and two are in pain or broken.

I should say now that I've already given both of my arms to our daughter. They attempt to soothe, to remove some of her burden. She is unmarried and has no children and works too hard. She's in her thirties, which she sees as being very old. It is not of course, but on the other hand every age is old when you know how fast it all goes, and that is something you only see when you get really impossibly old. I wish she would enjoy herself more. She is deeply afraid of being alone all her life, so she works to buy things to help her forget that. It is a fear that takes my breath away, that potential loneliness. It is unjust. She is brilliant and kind and loving and beautiful and wants a partner and I can't provide that for her. Who will love her best when we are gone? Who will give her Christmas gifts and stay overnight in the hospital with her if she's sick? Who will call her first if there's a natural disaster? Who will her own arm reach out to when she feels unsteady? So I gave her both my arms.

Still, I fear that something is very wrong with the construction of the human psyche. The 'I' has such a yearning to be 'we.' What I'm saying is, we shouldn't feel so separate unless we were meant to love that separation. And when I think that, that a mistake has been made in the building of this world, I am even more afraid that this universe is not predisposed to be kindly toward us. You can say all you want about the loneliness masking a yearning toward God, or that it is a proof of God's existence, but why create a want for something you could so freely give?

Anyway, when my third heart felt her despair and fear, I gave her both my arms. And while I told her, too, that even with a partner you are still alone, I think I may be lying. I'm not sure of this, but I think I may be. I have been very lucky in that regard though, and I don't think this is true of many.

Before I met my husband, I often had that existential fear that my daughter feels, and I thought it was as likely that the mind would go on after death as not, but that it might not be a pretty thing. That there was no reason to believe that the mind would not float around in space in absolute eternal terror, with no one to share it. (See above, about our construction.) This occasional terror comes to me still, but I know that when the terror comes I can reach someone to steady me. I somehow thought that marriage guaranteed that at least someone would be floating with you even after death, that there would be pillow talk in deep space, and I may have imparted that odd belief to our daughter.

Of course, she has a dog, and that's more than helpful. It is. I know about dogs.

She wants a child even more than she wants a partner, though, and if no partner presents him or herself, she will probably buy one (a child) if she can raise the funds. If she can't, her father and I will probably give her the money we have saved for the care of our aging bodies. I would rather spend that money on the care of a child who would be loved, though then our daughter would have to give up her own heart in ways she wouldn't now believe if I told her. But enough of this darkness.

Okay, there's one more minor thing.

I wish I could take away the heavy thighs that I gave her when she was born, as they are not currently in fashion and will probably not be in her lifetime, no matter how many body-positive messages we all receive. Her face is beautiful, and that was given to her by her father. Her father also has traditionally beautiful legs, with calves that will fit into any kind of boot, and thighs that would look good in the leather leggings that are in style this year or would look devastating in a large skirted dress if Fred Astaire, say, were to twirl them through the air while dancing.

Because of this, we are thinking of giving our daughter her father's legs for Christmas in the hope that she will be able to remove the ones she received from my genetic material (not that we're not grateful for the ten toes and her ability to walk) and attach the longer and thinner dancer's legs she will receive from her father (though her father was not a dancer and in fact has no sense of rhythm) without the hips then looking too wide. There will have to be a bit of skin modeling, but I do think it will work. I'm not sure what will happen to her shaving routine or whether the legs will rebel in some way. I would advise her to keep the old legs in case the new ones become unruly or she's in a diving accident or the shaving is too much trouble.

Lest you're thinking we take the temple of our bodies for granted, know that we are truly grateful for the blessings of our bodies, and we feed and exercise them and we only started giving parts of them away once the usual things didn't seem like quite enough.

When they first came to our house as adult children, we

would hand them bags of clementines and apples as they left, sometimes boxes of cereal we got 'two for one' we said, an extra roast we happened to have made the day before and had lying around, books we thought they might need for mid-course corrections, some spare twenty-dollar bills. I remember looking around in such a panic for things to hand them every time they left our house. We did this for a few years until we realized that what we were really saying was *take my arms, my soul, take everything you need!*

When our son gets up to leave (he and his father have watched half a basketball game on television, leaping up to shout when their team scores, the arm hitting the floor with its hand when the other team makes a basket, as my husband would have done on the chair had he been sitting on it and had the arm still been connected) we have to remind the boy to take the arm.

He picks it up and gives it a sniff, holds it up to his ear like a telephone. He tries holding it like a back scratcher to ease an itch. That seems to please him. We watch him throw the arm in the trunk of his car and drive away. We hope he remembers it's in there.

It was a good visit, my husband says, and he hugs my torso with the arm he has left. We both feel stretching rubber band pain in our chests as our other hearts drive away from us.

For the rest of the day we deconstruct every sentence that had come from his mouth, looking for clues to any sadness. If only he would give us a bit of his brain. It's not too much to ask in exchange. Just enough to know what he's seeing and dreaming about now. If he has desires, we would fulfill them if we could, though not all desires are fulfillable by parents. See the paragraph above about our daughter.

When Christmas comes, our daughter is delighted (we think) with the legs. She offers her father her own legs in exchange, and he tries them on. The proportions are all wrong on him, of course, though the longer legs on our daughter seem to make her happy. I will have to get used to this, I think. I liked her the way she was, truly, but now her body does look more in fashion. My husband tells the daughter to keep both pairs of legs in case she ever needs a spare, and she says she will. I give our son my hair, because his is rapidly disappearing and mine is thick. I had it cut right before the holidays in a style I thought might suit him. My mother had passed her hair along to me when I was born. She had enough for two. I laughed to myself at the thought and I had to remove my tongue to keep from making a stupid joke that might upset him (heirloom! I felt coming up from my throat, heirloom!) and so my tongue spent early Christmas evening in my jewelry box, fascinated by the differing surface temperature and texture between a garnet and an opal.

The children and my husband said the Yorkshire pudding was delicious, and the gravy, and the standing rib roast and mashed potatoes and the peas and the pear-and-mayonnaise salad and the rolls and butter and the cinnamon apple pie. When dinner was over and they were stuffed and drinking spiked coffee by the lighted tree, the children put the dishes in the dishwasher and I brought my tongue out of hiding to eat a few leftovers. By then my giddiness from the pre-dinner rum punch and wine had calmed a bit, and I could hold my tongue when necessary. When I joined them by the tree, I didn't ask where the son's girlfriend was. By then I was positive she'd broken his heart. I could feel the shards of it in my own chest as we waited for his to grow back in. The heart is regenerative, like the liver, but it scars a bit each time.

When the children left, they took two of my husband's legs, the other one of his arms, and my hair. And still, sigh, we worried that we hadn't given them enough. When they were gone with their gifts, my husband sat in the light of the tree and the television set. He looked quite a bit like the pears we'd had for dinner, truth be told.

That night we slept side by side, with my breasts pressing into his back. My legs spread out where his used to be. We were warm together, and it was a cold night. Do you think they'll appreciate what we gave them? my husband asked. Oh probably not, I said, but no matter. I reminded him of the attic and the china cabinet and linen closet where we stored appendages of our own parents and grandparents. In early years, we could hear them conferring, talking about us needlessly. It had never occurred to us, for some reason, to bring them out and use them ourselves. We could use them now, certainly, but they'd been silent for years and besides, we seemed to be doing fine. I had complicated feelings about using them, feelings I couldn't quite untangle. Are we doing the wrong thing? my husband asked me, crippling ourselves this way? I suppose, I said. In a way it's selfish of us, he said.

Perhaps, I said.

For the next few days, we learned how to get along

without four arms and two legs and one head of hair. We managed. There's a lot you can do with your teeth, and we had one of those smart devices with our credit card number already inserted, so we could ask it to order food and have it delivered to our house. And we had a dog of course, a large sweet golden mix with weak hips and a wolf's blue eyes. We kept the Christmas lights on all day and went to bed early as the days were short. From what we could tell, our son's heart seemed to be healing some, our daughter's was still overflowing but not choking her. My husband and I watched old movies together during the day, wrapped in blankets.

On Twelfth Night there was an ice storm and a full moon. Time to turn off the festive lights, which was always sad. At midnight we turned them off, but the windows were all a deep blue, the moonlight almost as strong as winter sunlight, but grayed and delicate.

Let's go outside, my husband said, and our dog brought us our coats and helped us drape them over our shoulders. We have levers for doorknobs, and the dog has always known how to open them. The sled, I told the dog, and he went to the side of the house and pulled it from underneath a bush by the frozen rope that was attached to it. I sat down in the foyer and used my feet to slide my husband's body down the steps and onto the waiting wooden sled. The dog pulled the sled down the driveway and toward the empty street. I walked behind for a bit and then found I could sit behind my husband on the sled with my feet stretched out and the dog, bless his soul, kept pulling us over the glistening ice.

The ice in the trees was like diamonds, in places like tinsel, the moon was so very beautiful and bright. The tree branches clicked together, metallic sounding, like wind chimes.

You know, my husband said to me, I think I've given all I can. We were going fast now, the dog's feet flying, despite his painful hips. I know you have, I said into my husband's red-dening ears. I wish he'd worn a hat.

They didn't ask for any of it of course, he said.

And didn't really need it I guess, I said.

It's the way it goes, he said, isn't it? We couldn't help it.

But selfish of us, as you said. And they probably don't like to see us like this, I said.

I rested my head on my husband's shoulder. The wind. The silver night, heavy limbs crashing deep in the woods from the weight of the ice, the sound of glass breaking. We glided on. In some northern climates, the young ones push the older ones out into the ocean on an ice floe, I reminded him.

So you've often said, he reminded me.

A night like this, I said. That's the way I'd like to go.

Such love there is in the universe, how much it hurts, he said.

It didn't have to be made this way, did it? I say.

Of course not, he said.

The sky was so clear, we could actually see stars. Dying, colliding stars, I said, and I wanted to reach out to them.

Such light, my husband said, such beauty.

My husband has more faith in the basic goodness of the universe.

The dog's breath was like smoke, his tail wagging, head

high. He was proud of pulling us through the world. He only stopped once, to pee against a frosted stone, the stream hissing against the ice.

For a second, I felt the familiar sense of falling and slipping through some vast darkness. Just let go, I thought I heard the dog say as he picked up speed again. And it will feel like flying.

Can't I give you anything to help you run? I asked the dog, as long as we were talking.

It's all good, the dog said.

Eventually the dog circled back toward our house. When we arrived, my husband stood up from the sled on two legs. I stood up and greeted him with new arms and he hugged me with his two new arms as though it were nothing at all to have them again. My hair was as long as it had been when I was a girl. And my heart wasn't separate from my body, though it wasn't in my chest exactly. It was in my fingers and my skin and eyes and in the ice and crashing trees, and I could see through my husband's eyes and my children's and through the dog's eyes and I could taste the snow and for a moment I believed that everything was just as it should be.

Hunger

I'M DRIVING DOWN THE STREET and I have an overwhelming urge to take a bite out of my steering wheel, so I do. The steering wheel is black plastic, more like a toy car's steering wheel than the faux leather-covered wheels my parents had when I was growing up. I don't know what's come over me. It doesn't taste particularly good, and it makes a loud crunching sound against my teeth. It's like the crispy version of a plastic pen, a familiar though not entirely unpleasant taste. It's hard to swallow, but I swallow it and take another bite.

I have to say that I like the sound it makes as I eat it. It fills my head with sound, like when you eat ice. I'm aware that my mouth is filled with shards of black plastic, but somehow it doesn't seem to cause any harm to my gums or teeth or to my esophagus.

Of course I'm worried about the steering because I eat and eat the wheel until I've gnawed it down to nothing and at the end I'm attempting to drive the car by holding onto the post with both hands. It's not an easy thing to steer the car this way. In fact, it's impossible. Luckily, I'm in a small town on a Saturday night and there's no traffic and the auto parts store is open, blaring light.

It's a dark night, no stars, and I drive right into the garage bay which is connected to the storefront by a sliding glass door, which tonight is open as there are no engines running in the bay. In the waiting room, red and yellow and fluorescent lighting and cash registers and stacks of luscious clipboards with pens hanging from the clips on strings.

Some faceless guy in a mechanic's jumpsuit doesn't seem to mind that I've driven straight through the garage and into the store. He finds a replacement wheel behind the counter. It's like he expected me. I'm pleased to not feel embarrassed and to not have to explain that I ate the first wheel, though I'm sure he's seen my kind before. In fact, I'd noticed a car in the garage that appeared to have big bites taken out of the chassis. As I looked closer, though, I saw it was just the ordinary hunger of oxidation, that lacy rust.

The mechanic pops open the hood on my car, and I ponder sucking the fluid from the battery, putting a straw in the lovely chartreuse of the antifreeze. Suicidal thoughts, those, so I consider instead stuffing my mouth with wires or snapping the axle and eating it like a sugar stick. Or the headlamps? The combination of the glass and metal and the filaments might do for a snack. But nothing, I realize, would give me the pure pleasure of the steering wheel. It's not a generalized hunger for cars, I tell myself, and that comforts me. Somewhat. I haven't gone completely mad. The plastic-ey crackle of the wheel is what I want.

But why? I'm in a waiting room, waiting, and I have time to think a bit. (Should I have engaged in thought before I ate the steering wheel? I can hear you asking. Of course, though my desire was so great that thought in all its thoughtiness would have been helpless against the desire.) But I realize that my hunger could have chosen something else. Medicine bottles or street lights. Tree branches or aluminum siding. I have never wanted to take a bite of the cup holder or a handful of change from between the seats or, for that matter, I have never wanted to devour the head rest. Why this particular desire?

For the moment when the steering wheel was inside of me, of course, I had no way of controlling the car. Is that what I wanted? To lose control? Did I want to drive headlong over an embankment or into a tree? If so, I think I would have been driving faster. I wouldn't have been in a town or near an auto parts store where, so conveniently, a man handed me an even better wheel than the one I'd just consumed, a wheel that even then was making my mouth water. It was right there waiting, as soon as I drove into the warmth of the store.

Maybe it was the store I needed? When I was by myself in the car I felt, I'll admit, a bit lost. A bit at the mercy of my compulsions. The light and the companionship of the garage were welcome.

Or maybe it was the anxiety of choice I wanted to rid myself of. Left or right? This way or that? Day in and day out, year after year, I drove in my little rat's maze. Grocery store. Drugstore. Work. Home. But in what order? And what if I wanted to break out of that maze, as I sometimes did. What was keeping me from driving north, crossing the border into Canada, heading through to Alaska and driving across the Bering Strait (on ice? a ferry?) into Siberia and on to St. Petersburg with its pink and lavender winter darkness. And down to Yalta, perhaps, then a trip to Italy and to the town in Greece with all the blue doors and then to Morocco all salmon-colored, the odor of saffron. Even as I imagine St. Petersburg and Yalta and Italy and Greece and the beautiful sunlit gardens of Morocco, I wonder why I was given these visions and neither the courage nor the money nor the strength to follow through.

Maybe my hunger was for color. I feel myself sinking into the beauty of the colored world, the northern lights, the phosphorescent foam of the Mediterranean, the beauty like a dreamscape beckoning and the dailiness of my gray life moving so quickly by me, and all the love and responsibilities of the life I've built. I am no nomad, no traveler. So maybe I ate the wretched steering wheel to get rid of the visions.

Would that it were that simple. As an explanation, it doesn't suit entirely. It's simply not sufficient. It doesn't account for the pleasure of the dreams or of the dreams held in such perfect balance with the pleasure of my life as I've built it, the pleasure of the conflict, and most of all does not account for the pleasure of the devouring.

(Though when I caught sight of myself in the rearview mirror as I was driving and eating I looked, to myself, for one second, like those grotesque paintings of the devil with helpless humans dripping from his gargoyle mouth.)

Anyway, as I sat in the warmth of the waiting room waiting for my steering wheel to be replaced, already growing ravenous though a bit nauseated by the smell of tires, I thought about it nutritionally, scientifically. There could, I suppose, be a missing nutrient, one found in plastic. Throughout my life (and I think I'm not alone in this) I've loved to pry the little black plug off the top of Bic pens. I prefer the plug to the caps, most of which I lose anyway. I've had some major ink spillage because of these tendencies.

Am I alone in this? You pry the plug out with your teeth and then, while you're taking notes or whatever with the pen, your hand moving almost independently of your desires, you chew on the plug. The trick is to make it last and not to swallow it, so you soft mouth it with your front teeth and move it to the molars only as you decide to stick your tongue in the pen's tube and then roll the plug back into the pen, lightly chewing it back into shape to make it fit. And then, after a while, you suck it out again and put it back and so on until the point when it is so misshapen that you could not possibly reinsert it. Even then, though, you don't swallow it. My technique is always to remove the plug delicately like you might remove a small bone or olive pit at a dinner party, with many glances to make sure no one is watching.

Why is the plug even there? I mean there in the pen. What function does it serve? Does the cylinder of ink need air in order to flow properly? One of the pleasures of life is that there is always so much to think about and attempt to understand. I don't understand the un-curious, though often I envy them. You pick up a pen, you write a few lines, and you're done. You get in the car and turn the wheel in the proper direction, and you don't think about eating it. Right now the issue that is most pressing is whether or not I will be able to flow properly myself in the stream of traffic, how I will get anyplace at all if I keep eating steering wheels.

I will soon find out, as it appears the mechanic has replaced the wheel, and it appears that our relationship has run its course. I pay him for the wheel and for his service and I pay him for a second wheel because, you know, because. He places it in the trunk of my car with the jack and the spare tire.

A little wave, and I'm off.

Perhaps it is time now for some confessions. First, I am for the most part happiest in my car. When I am told by my smartphone that I have reached my destination, I outsmart it by driving around the block or several blocks. I generally do not want to reach my destination.

Second, I must have complete quiet in the car. I do not listen to music. I listen to my thoughts.

Third, I am a far better driver without passengers.

Fourth, I like to drive myself, that is, to never be a passenger.

Fifth, I am of course (in case you're wondering) very concerned about our use of fossil fuel, and I feel awful about using so much of it for such nonutilitarian reasons such as driving aimlessly around. And still, I drive aimlessly around.

Sixth, I love the comfort of the shell of an automobile around me. I feel like a turtle or a crustacean. It is an exoskeleton, the car. It is my house.

Seventh. Oh, there is no seventh.

I assume my hunger has something to do with fear. If I eat the car, I will not drive to Morocco, worrying my family unduly. I can hear them now: Where will you stay? How will you live? Will you be raped or will you be sold as a sex slave or will you be beheaded? Or shot or speared as an infidel of some sort? These are the first things that go through my family's mind when I talk of driving out of state, even if I remain inside this country. There are, in fact, no other outcomes in their minds but these. And I can't say that I'm immune to their concerns.

So I leave the store with my new shiny wheel, my hands at ten and two. I reach into my purse to find lip gloss and accidentally my hand grazes against my phone. In a second I hear my daughter's voice from inside my purse yelling Mom! and, as she tells me later, she watches my hand as it fumbles for the lip gloss. Cherry flavored. Mom!

I pull her rectangular face out of my bag and she looks relieved. I felt like I was being buried alive, she says and then asks, Where are you? I'm driving, I say, and there's an uncanny valley sort of blip in her face as she continues doing whatever she was doing when I accidentally called her. She seems to be in the kitchen, boiling water. It's not the daughter I remember. She's not looking at me, but then it's part of what you do when you talk to the rectangle of plastic that contains your loved one. You don't look directly at the person. It can't seem like a real conversation where you look someone in the eye because you're not looking at real eyes.

Happy Birthday by the way, she says to me.

I'd forgotten, I say. I truly had forgotten how old I had become. Really, I had. I'd gone the whole day without remembering, I say to her.

I'm sorry I forgot to call, she says.

I thought my phone was dead, I say.

I was so busy, she says, today.

I know, I say, your sisters too. I would never even place a straw in your way, I add. This is your time, I say.

I was thinking about Daddy today, she says.

I miss him too, I say. He has been dead six months now. I understand how painful it is for my children. What can I say to them?

Still, this morning and all day I was alone with the thoughts chattering, as they always do, inside my head. As though I am the center of the universe. I see. I do. I think. I'm tired. I hurt. At one time it was easy for me to believe I was the center, as is true, admit it, for all of us. I love. You love me. This house is our house, and in that house our thoughts merging with each other's like globules of water meeting. Expanding. Then dividing. I am smaller now than I was then, smaller than I ever was before.

Oh, dearest darling, I say to the beloved child, oh dearest girl, I say, you won't believe what I just did.

But she has clicked off. On to her own life. I pull to the side of the road and pop the trunk. Inside the dark place, among the detritus, I see the wheel.

Acknowledgments

With deepest gratitude to my writing group friends. Couldn't have written these stories without your editing, your friendship, the deadlines. To Dan Wakefield, for his belief in and encouragement of these stories. Thanks to all my amazing colleagues and students in the Butler English Department for your inspiration and kindness and particularly to Mindy Dunn, Alessandra Lynch, Andrew Levy, Hilene Flanzbaum, Jason Goldsmith, Dan Barden, and Carol Reeves, for reading or listening to and encouraging early drafts of these stories. My gratitude to the editors of the magazines that first published these stories. Thanks to FC2, to Michael Martone for the heads-up about the deadline for the Catherine Doctorow Prize, to Joanna Ruocco for her support, and to Shelley Jackson for choosing this book. To my graduate student Andrea Donderi, for her brilliant essay on endings. I relied heavily on her insights in "The Dead." I am beyond grateful.

I couldn't have written this book without the love of my life, Ken Neville, and the support and love of our children and of our dear friends and extended family.

Thanks to my husband's family, in particular Shirley Neville Brown, for their strength and for their stories about the formation of Camp Atterbury. Shirley is a far better writer than I am about these things, and the articles she found in the archives of the Columbus paper appear in the story "Transfiguration."

And finally, while The Town of Whispering Dolls isn't a real place in the same way that characters are never real people (but are made of images gathered from perceptions and from dreams and fantasy and from other books) I will say that the town I'm imagining was inspired by Edinburgh, Garden City, Columbus, New Castle, Muncie, South Bend, Gas City, Corydon, New Harmony, Evansville, Knightstown, Connersville, Hagerstown, Austin, and who knows how many other current and former small industrial towns. If this imagined place exists, it is someplace south of Indianapolis.

Stories in this collection appeared, in a slightly different form, in the following periodicals: "Hunger," the *Missouri Review*; "Here," *Southwest Review*; "Grotto," *DIAGRAM*; "Shock and Awe," *Gargoyle*; "Game Night," *The Collagist*; "Resurrection," *DIAGRAM*; "The Warhol Girl," *Valparaiso Fiction Review*; "Restaurant With the Glass Lamps," the *Missouri Review*; "Parting," *Gargoyle*; "She Drinks Too Much of It," *Winesburg, Indiana: A Fork River Anthology*; "The Wind Farm at Night," *The Collagist*; "Plume," *Four Way Review*; and "Copies," *Sycamore Review*.